A Year Without Autumn

Also by Liz Kessler

Philippa Fisher's Fairy Godsister
Philippa Fisher and the Dream-Maker's Daughter
Philippa Fisher and the Fairy's Promise

The Tail of Emily Windsnap
Emily Windsnap and the Monster from the Deep
Emily Windsnap and the Castle in the Mist
Emily Windsnap and the Siren's Secret

Emily Windsnap's Fin-tastic Friendship Book

A Year Without Autumn

LIZ KESSLER

CANDLEWICK PRESS

Copyright © 2011 by Liz Kessler

First published in Great Britain by Orion Children's Books, a division of the Orion Publishing Group

First U.S. edition 2011

Library of Congress Cataloging-in-Publication Data

Kessler, Liz.
A year without Autumn / Liz Kessler. — 1st U.S. ed.
p.   cm.
Summary: Twelve-year-old Jenni's much-anticipated vacation with her family and best friend Autumn goes awry when an old elevator transports her to a future in which everything has changed, and she must not only return to her time but find a way to prevent what she has seen from coming true.
ISBN 978-0-7636-5595-2
[1. Time travel — Fiction. 2. Best friends — Fiction. 3. Friendship — Fiction. 4. Family life — England — Fiction. 5. Vacations — Fiction. 6. England — Fiction.] I. Title.
PZ7.K4842Ye 2011
[Fic] — dc22   2010045957

11 12 13 14 15 16 RRC 10 9 8 7 6 5 4 3 2 1

Printed in the Crawfordsville, IN, U.S.A.

This book was typeset in Perpetua.

Candlewick Press
99 Dover Street
Somerville, Massachusetts 02144

visit us at www.candlewick.com

This book is dedicated to Judith Elliott, to say thank you for eight years of sharing your wisdom, patience, ideas, kindness, and inspiration. It's been a privilege to work with you and to learn from the best.

And in today already walks tomorrow.

— Friedrich von Schiller

$\mathcal{S}top$ the car!"

"What?" Dad swivels around in his seat. The car swerves.

"Good grief, Tom!" Mom squeals, gripping her armrest as she pulls a wad of tissues out of her purse.

"Stop the car!" I repeat. It's going to be too late in a minute. I grab the tissues and shove them over Craig's mouth.

Dad pulls over just in time, and Craig lurches out of his seat, runs to the side of the road, and doubles over.

The car stinks for the rest of the trip.

I sniff pointedly. "Mmm, get a load of that fresh country air."

"I didn't even do it in the car, Jenni," Craig mumbles as I open my window and stick my head out.

Welcome to the Green family vacation. Green by name, green by nature, if my little brother's face is anything to go by. Mom's isn't much better, either. But then she is eight months pregnant, so she's got an excuse at least — especially when Dad's behind the wheel.

Honestly, I could predict this journey with my eyes closed. It's the same every year. An hour of Dad driving too fast around the bendy back roads, during which Mom will ask him to slow down at least ten times and Craig will puke at least once, followed by three hours of crawling up the highway with ten trillion other families who have suddenly realized there's only one more week of summer vacation left.

Then we'll arrive at our time-share, which will look exactly the same as it does every year, and exactly the same as all the other condos at Riverside Village: big open-plan living room and kitchen, both beige and cream, both spotlessly clean and tidy. No dirty stains on the brown leather sofa. No finger marks on the TV. Microwave, toaster oven, dish rack, fruit bowl. Everything labeled and sitting neatly in its place, checked off in the Guest File. In the place it's been when we've come into the condo on the last Saturday of August every year, ever since I can remember.

But we like it like that. That's the thing about my

family. We like order; we like to be in the right place at the right time. We don't like surprises or change very much. I guess that's why we have a time-share — so we know exactly what to expect. Same thing every year. I could even tell you which leaves will have started to turn red. It's always the same ones. Every year.

"Perfect," Dad says with a satisfied nod as he pulls into the parking lot. "Fourteen hundred hours." Which is two o'clock for normal people. The exact time we're allowed into the condo.

"Right on time," Mom says with a smile. "Well done, darling."

That's what they like to be, my mom and dad. Right on time.

There's a strange comfort as we unpack the car and settle in. It's sort of like when winter comes and you dig out those big fluffy sweaters that you haven't thought about all year but you suddenly remember you love, and you're glad you've got the chance to wear them again.

There's a huge TV in the middle of the living room that swivels all the way around, so you can watch it from anywhere in the room. And there's a bed that folds out from the wall, which you'd never notice unless you knew it was there; it's like something you'd see in a James Bond movie. Not that we ever use it—but just knowing it's there feels exotic and mysterious. And there's always a tray of candy on the table to welcome you. I let Craig dive into the candy while I take my bags to the room we share so I can get the best bed by the window.

I hate sharing a room with Craig. For one thing, he snores and grunts all night, and I have to creep around in the dark when I come to bed so I don't wake him up. And then he babbles about all sorts of nonsense in the morning, telling me about his dreams of monsters made from jelly. And for another—

"Watch out, sis."

Right on cue, the little monster barges in, plonks his backpack on the other bed, and starts pulling out its contents.

Approximately thirty seconds later, his bed and half the floor space are completely buried under a pile of clothes, a small mountain of LEGOs, five packs of candy, three pairs of dirty sneakers, and about fifty model cars, buses, and tractors.

"Done!" he says, shoving his backpack under the bed and folding his arms.

"Done?" I say. "Done what?"

"Unpacked," he says simply. He grabs a handful of LEGOs and heads for the door.

Once he's gone, I stare at the bomb site he's left behind and take a deep breath.

Like I said, I *hate* sharing a room with Craig.

I guess I'm quite mature for my age. Everyone says so. "Twelve going on twenty," my dad says. I'm the oldest in my class at school and the oldest child in the family. Sometimes it gets a bit annoying always having to be the older, sensible one — but I suppose that's just how I am.

There's a *thump-thump-thump* along the hallway, and Craig appears in the room again.

He grabs another handful of LEGOs, then rifles through various jean pockets till he finds a bag of candy left behind goodness knows how many eons ago. He picks a lemon ball from the bag and hands it to me. While I'm looking at it and wondering exactly where it's been, he unwraps a chewy lollipop for himself.

"What goes 'Ha-ha, bonk'?" he reads from the wrapper.

"I don't know," I say.

"A man laughing his head off."

There's a pause as he lets the joke digest. A second later, he falls forward on his bed and guffaws in his inimitable half-choke/half-hyena giggle that I can't help smiling at, despite my irritation.

That's the thing with Craig. He's the only person who really annoys me, the only one who can make me want to scream with frustration, but then sometimes he can make me laugh so much I cry. The only other person who can do that is Autumn. She's the funniest person in the world and the brightest and smartest and all-around fabulousest! And she's my best friend!

Dad pokes his head around the door. "Fancy a walk, Jenni bear?"

"Yeah, why not?" I reply, wincing slightly at the pet name he's had for me since I was about three. I haven't got the heart to ask him not to use it; he'd be all hurt, and that would be even worse than being called baby names.

I put the last of my clothes into a drawer and shove my backpack into the closet. On the way downstairs, I pull my hair into a ponytail with a scrunchie. It's driving me crazy — it falls all over my face in loopy ringlets if I don't pull it back.

"Depriving us of your lovely curly locks again?" Dad says with a wink as I join him and Mom in the living room. If they had their way, I'd let it grow down to my knees, but I'm determined to get it cut, once I can persuade them it's not the end of the world. They're scared it'll be the start of a slippery slope. I've tried to explain that a change of hairstyle doesn't automatically lead to two-inch-thick makeup, multiple piercings, and a tattooed neck, but they're not convinced yet. So I just smile and discreetly pull my scrunchie a little bit tighter.

Craig is sprawled out on the living-room floor, making an incredibly complex-looking robot out of LEGOs. Mom's propped up on the sofa with a magazine and a cup of tea.

"Take it easy," Dad says, reaching over to kiss her forehead and pat her eight-months-pregnant tummy.

He ruffles Craig's hair on his way across the room. "See you later, kid," he says. Craig doesn't look up. He's concentrating too hard on the robot, his tongue poking tightly out the side of his mouth.

Dad takes my hand while we walk along the gravelly path. I stop myself from pulling away and reminding him that I'm not five years old. Instead, I let him hold it for a minute, and then pretend I have to scratch my neck so I can let go.

We walk past the second building of the complex. Together with ours, it's the modern part of Riverside

Village. These two buildings were added on only about ten years ago. The other two buildings have been here for nearly a hundred years. One of them, the reception building, is ahead of us, an elongated cottage with a thatched roof and bushy green ivy all over the walls. Autumn's building is across the way from reception and the grandest of the lot. Autumn's family has one of the fancy condos on the second floor. They were updated at the same time that our building was added, and they all have huge bedrooms, massive terraces, and Jacuzzis in all three bedrooms!

We're just walking between the two buildings when the sound of a loud horn behind us nearly makes me jump out of my skin. I spin around to see a red Porsche roaring toward us.

"Autumn!" I run over to meet Autumn and her family as they pull up in the parking lot.

Autumn waves madly from the tiny backseat, where she and her little brother, Mikey, are both scrunched up with their knees practically behind their ears, suitcases on their laps, and most of the window space taken up with bags.

Autumn's dad is an artist, and her mom is the manager at the gallery where he sells his work. He bought the car as a present for himself when they sold one of his paintings for a whopping amount. He wouldn't tell us how much it went for, but Mrs. Leonard said it could have bought them a new kitchen. So that was what he bought as *her* present when they sold the next painting!

Autumn's parents are totally fabulous. It's always crazy at their house. Lots of people are always coming by to visit, and her parents are always throwing dinner parties and having loud conversations where everyone talks at once, and no one ever tells Autumn or Mikey it's time for bed, and Autumn gets to do things like bake bread and paint on the walls. We even helped her dad make cocktails once for a party they were having. That was so cool. Bright red-and-green drinks, and we served them to all their artist friends in glasses that we frosted with pink sugar.

Their house always smells of incense that they've brought back from some exotic vacation. I feel like I'm on vacation myself when I'm over there. It's *so* different from our house. Nothing changes from one day to the next at home, and nothing's ever a mess. Although I kind of like that, too. At least you know where you are.

I guess Autumn's folks must like having at least one week of the year where life is a bit more ordered.

I can't think of any other reason why they'd come to Riverside Village — except to see us, of course! Although I don't understand that one, either. Sometimes I wonder why Autumn would want me as her best friend. I'm nowhere near as interesting as she is. Whenever I tell her that, she just laughs and says I'm being stupid and we're best friends forever. And even though I still don't get why she chose me, I know it's true. She'd never lie to me.

Mrs. Leonard peels herself out of the car and smiles at me. "Hello, Jenni love," she says. "How's your mom?" She comes over and kisses me on both cheeks.

"She's fine," I say, blushing at the exotic greeting. "She's back at the condo with Craig."

"Putting her feet up for once," Dad adds.

Autumn's mom and my mom are best friends, too. While Autumn and I were splatting paint at each other and sharing books way back in kindergarten, our moms were swapping recipes and gossiping about our teachers outside on the playground. Dad and Mr. Leonard have become friends as well.

Autumn and Mikey tumble out of the car. Mikey doesn't look up from the video game he's more or less attached to. Autumn runs around the car to me, red hair flying.

"Jenni!" she yells, and we fling our arms around each other and jump up and down.

Mr. Leonard gets out of the car and gently closes the door behind him. "Watch the car, girls," he says, warding us away from his pride and joy. He reaches out to shake Dad's hand and nods over at us. "Wouldn't think this pair only saw each other yesterday, would you?" he says with a smile.

"*Yesterday?*" Dad replies in mock horror. "But that's a whole *day* ago. That's practically a lifetime!"

"Ha-ha, very funny," Autumn retorts. "For your information, there are a *million* things Jenni and I need to share since yesterday. Aren't there, Jenni?"

I giggle and grin at Autumn. "At *least* a million," I say. "Maybe even a million and a half."

"Well, they'll all have to wait because I need a hand with these," Mr. Leonard says as he pulls the last of their suitcases out of the car.

I stare at the pile of matching designer suitcases next to the Porsche.

"How on earth did you get it all in?" I ask.

Autumn beams at me. "It's a clown car!" she says,

her eyes glinting with mischievous delight. She does a silly walk while humming circus music.

Mikey looks up for the first time. "A clown car?" he says. "Where?"

Mrs. Leonard strokes his cheek. "Your sister's joking, sweetheart," she says. "It's not a clown car. It's a Porsche. Otherwise known as a middle-aged man's midlife crisis."

Mikey screws his nose up and looks at his sister. "What's that?" he says.

Autumn smiles affectionately at her brother. "Just boring grown-up stuff. Nothing for us to worry about, kid," she says, ruffling his hair.

Mikey shrugs off the ruffle and goes back to his game.

"Little brothers," she says with a dramatic sigh. "Don't you just love them?"

She's joking, but I know she means it, really. Mikey brings out Autumn's love and protectiveness like no one else can, just like Craig does with me. We love them to death — but we wouldn't tell them in a million years!

Mikey's two years older than Craig, so they're not best friends or anything, but they hang out a bit when we're here, which makes Craig feel very grown-up.

Although "hanging out" might be a slight exaggeration. It's generally a case of Mikey sitting around playing his latest video game and Craig being given the privilege of watching. But it works for them.

"OK, come on," Dad says, reaching for my hand and pulling me away. "Let's leave so they can unpack. I'm sure the million and a half things can last till later. See you guys at the welcome meeting?"

The welcome meeting is when the Riverside Village people tell us what activities there will be during the week. There's a little movie theater inside the reception building where they show a different film every night, and there are always lots of other things going on every day: everything from bird-watching to hot-air balloon rides.

"Absolutely!" Autumn's parents say in unison.

Autumn jumps to attention and salutes. "Aye, aye, Cap'n. See you there," she says, and blows me a kiss as she runs off to help her parents with their bags.

I can't help wondering what crazy activity Autumn will rope me into at this year's welcome meeting. She always tries to drag me off on some zany trip—and I usually end up going. I can't imagine saying no to Autumn over anything. I think it's got something to do with the gleam in her eyes and the smile on her face.

You always know that if she suggests something, it'll probably be half crazy, half goofy, but one hundred percent better than anything else — as long as you do it with her. She could even make bricklaying seem exciting! Don't ask me how; she just could.

If it wasn't for Autumn, I'd avoid any of the adventure trips. I prefer to visit museums. I know that sounds boring, but I don't think it is. Museums open my mind, and my imagination runs away with itself. All those old objects and strange artifacts make me think about all the people who used them and wonder what their lives were like.

And Dad usually drags us out on at least two mammoth walks while we're here. Walking is Dad's big thing. That and writing. He's — well, he'd say he's a writer, but that's just because he's been going to this creative-writing class and the teacher told them they all have to call themselves writers. She says that's the first step. Personally, I'd have thought the first step would be putting words to paper, but that's just my opinion.

He's really a math teacher. Assistant head of math at the same school I go to! How embarrassing is *that*? Actually, sixth grade wasn't too bad. I wasn't in his class, and as long as I never get him as my homeroom teacher, I don't mind *too* much. Mom's a therapist at the university in the next town. She doesn't talk much about her work—she pretty much pleads the Fifth every time someone asks her anything about it.

Dad and I take a walk beside the river. A great big swan and two fluffy brown cygnets are paddling in the water, swept along sideways by the rush of the current. It's flowing by faster than I've ever seen it.

"The river's high," Dad says swinging my arm as we walk.

"It's in a hurry," I say.

Dad stands back from me and stares for a second. "That's good," he says. "I like it." Then he gets out his notebook and scribbles down what I said. You have to be careful around Dad. When he's in one of his "creative" moods, pretty much anything you say could get jotted down and saved up for the day he writes his best-selling novel.

I say "novel." What it really is, if we're honest, is a notebook that he's had for years, stuffed with scraps of paper and napkins where he's scribbled tiny half-ideas and the odd line of poetry.

He says that's the mark of a real novelist, the fact that he carries this notebook around. I've tried telling him the mark of a real novelist is a real novel, but he just closes his eyes and smiles to himself in that way that means he knows the real truths about life and I'll understand when I'm older.

I write, too, but only in my diary. I've never shown it to anyone. I'd die before doing that, although I sometimes read snippets to Autumn. She always points out hidden meanings in what I've written, picking up on every little thing to tell me something about myself that I hadn't noticed when I wrote it. She makes me sound much more interesting than I really am!

Autumn doesn't keep a diary. She wouldn't have the patience. Everything she does has to involve moving, preferably outside, even when it's raining. She can't bear to sit still. She goes rock climbing with her dad and takes a weird dance class that a friend of her mom's runs. She's tried to get me to go to it with her, but I can't dance. I've tried, but I just freeze up. I turn so stiff, I feel as though I'm wearing a suit of armor.

You might be wondering what exactly we have in common. I do, too, sometimes. But it's as if we're two different halves of one whole or something. I can talk to her about absolutely anything, and she's the same with me. We never get bored of each other's lives. We share everything — every last detail.

Dad and I stand watching the water foam and fight as it rushes to get under the bridge. A couple of boys in sneakers and shorts climb onto the wall, and we watch them prepare to jump into the swirling water.

"I tell you," Dad says, shaking his head as the first boy splashes loudly into the water, "if either of you kids ever thinks about doing that —"

"Don't worry, Dad," I say, laughing. "I wouldn't dream of it!" We have the same conversation every year. How he even thinks I might consider it, I don't know.

"GERONIMO!" Another splash as the next boy pounds into the river.

I shudder as we move on, down to the weir. One year we'd had a really hot summer, and the weir had completely dried up. You could see a wall running across the river, only a tiny layer of water covering it up. Autumn skipped across it and dared me to do the same.

I tried to say no, but like I said, Autumn doesn't really do "no." In the end, she held my hand and practically dragged me across. I clutched her hand so tightly, she had red marks from my nails in her palm for a week.

It felt amazing once we got to the other side, so I was glad she'd insisted — as I usually am. I'd never do something like that of my own accord, though. Never in a million years. It's not that I'm a complete wimp. It's just that, well, it's dangerous! It might *look* safe, but you never know what's underneath or how slippery it is, or if the river will suddenly change and you'll get washed away and knocked unconscious on the rocks below. Too risky by half, and the Green family doesn't do risky.

We like things to be ordered, safe, predictable. That's why we come here. It's *always* predictable here. At least it always has been up to now.

Dad points to the mist swirling above the weir as we pick our way across moss-covered rocks. The water's crashing down so hard, we have to shout to hear each other. It's like Niagara Falls.

"Not surprising after all the rain we've had this summer!" Dad yells in my ear.

I stand back as some of the spray splashes a rock below us. "Let's go back!" I shout.

We pass Mr. Andrews, one of Dad's friends, on the way back to the condo. I study the woods on the other side of the river as they chat. Row after row of tall, sturdy trees — they look proud and aloof, as if they know more than we do. They've seen it all. The leaves on a group of them have turned red. The same trees every year, just one small section of the woods. How do they do it? How do they know?

"Come on, cupcake." Dad nudges me, and I give Mr. Andrews a quick wave and an embarrassed smile as we set off. Will Dad *ever* realize I've grown out of his pet names? Will I ever have the heart to tell him?

We go into the rec center so Dad can book a squash court for him and Mr. Andrews. He never plays squash except when we're here; I don't know why he bothers. I watched a bit of his game once. He's really thin and spindly. He looked like a spider on ice, slipping about all over the court, crashing into walls, and coming away purple with bruises. Mr. Andrews had hardly built up a sweat.

Dad books the court for tomorrow afternoon and then stops to talk to the receptionist. I look around the shop while they talk. There's a rack of tiny work-out clothes and skimpy swimsuits and six shelves of chocolates and candy. I've never quite understood how these go together.

"Just a little surprise for your mom," Dad says, linking his arm through mine as he pockets a gift card for a facial.

It's their wedding anniversary tomorrow. Fifteen years. They still get all gooey about each other, and they hardly ever argue. They bicker sometimes, of course. But only as much as anyone's parents and about a hundred times less than Autumn's. *Their* arguments are like volcanic eruptions. One minute they're so laid-back they're practically lying down, and the next they're at each other's throats. Autumn says it's because they're artists. It's the creative temperament.

"If I could have your attention, please." Mr. Barraclough taps the side of his glass with a spoon, and the room gradually quiets down. Mr. Barraclough's the manager here. He's really tall, with a wavy mop of gray hair and blue eyes that always seem to shine without sparkling, if that makes sense.

He wears sharp suits and always has his shirt collar turned up. I think he looks like a cross between an old rock star and a really cool principal.

Everyone's at the welcome meeting, looking up at him and waiting to hear about the week's goodies. Well, everyone except Autumn's family. They aren't here yet — but that's no surprise. They're late to everything. I think they like to make an entrance.

Mom looks at the drinks and raises her eyebrows. "Champagne this year. What's that about?" She pats her stomach. "Shame I can't have any," she says. I grab three cups of orange juice for her, Craig, and myself as Dad helps himself to a glass of champagne and downs half of it in one gulp.

Mr. Barraclough has started talking again. "So, as this is my last year, I thought we'd do it up," he says.

"Bit young for retiring, aren't you?" a red-faced man at the side of the room calls out. "Or are we paying you too much?"

"I wish!" Mr. Barraclough says, half frowning, half smiling. "No, I just thought I'd do some traveling. See some of the world beyond Riverside Village," he adds. "I'm fifty this year. Can't put your life on hold forever." Then he stares out the window and pauses. For a moment, he seems to have forgotten about all of us. The pause is just starting to feel awkward when he coughs and raises his glass with a smile that looks really sad. You'd think he'd seem a little happier about leaving his job to go traveling.

"Anyway, I hope you all settle into your condos without any problems," he says. "I'm here whenever you need me, as are my staff. Try to remember, if it's a sink you need unblocking, there's Johnny and Rita and Pete, and if you need someone to share a long drink and chat with in the bar, you've got my number."

A few people laugh while Mr. Barraclough takes a sip of his champagne. "We've got a whole bunch of top-notch events planned for you this week, as always," he continues, "so please take your time to check out all the activities, sign up before it's too late, and, most of all, have a wonderful week. Thank you."

With that, he raises his glass and nods to a small round of applause.

Mom grabs my arm. "Come on. Let's see what they've got planned."

I grab a handful of dry-roasted peanuts and follow her to join the others crowding around a table that stretches down one side of the room. It's covered with leaflets and brochures and sign-up forms. Dad and Craig wander over to a board at the other side of the room. It shows pictures of a local steam train. That's another thing that happens every year. Craig's world would be turned upside down if we didn't have at least one ride on the steam train while we're here.

"Look. They haven't done a trip here before, have they?" Mom passes me a leaflet about a candle museum. "You can make your own candles," she adds.

I study the leaflet. There are pictures of candles shaped like mermaids and fairies and trees and all sorts of things. I imagine Autumn and me making matching candles and giving them to each other as presents. "It looks good," I agree.

Mom picks up the sign-up sheet. "They're doing a trip tomorrow afternoon. Shall I sign us up?"

"Yeah, great," I reply, glancing at the door for the twentieth time to see if Autumn's here yet.

A second later, Dad comes over, pulling Craig along by the hand. Craig's walking like a bowlegged cowboy; his pants are soaked.

"He knocked his drink over," Dad says. "I'll take him home to change. Back in a minute."

He pauses at the door to talk to someone who's just arrived. I peer around the corner. Yay! It's Autumn!

She screams my name so loud that half the room turns to see what's going on, then she runs over and squeezes me so tight that she practically knocks the wind out of me as her parents come in behind her. They're dressed in matching linen pants and bright tops: his baby blue, hers bright pink. Autumn's wearing old jeans and a red T-shirt with a white donkey in the middle. When they come in, the room changes, as though it was black-and-white before and they've flicked a switch that's turned it into color.

"Didn't you girls see each other about two hours ago?" Mom asks.

"Yeah, but we haven't had time to catch up on the two million things we need to tell each other yet," Autumn says.

"Two million? It was a million and a half at the last count," her mom says with a smile.

"That was two hours ago! There's more now!"

I laugh, but she's right. There's always so much I want to tell her. Just stupid things, stuff most people wouldn't bother with but I know she'll want to hear about.

"I suppose I know what you mean," Mom says, kissing Autumn's mom on the cheek and pulling her to one side while Autumn's dad goes over to speak to Mr. Barraclough.

"Let's see what they've got lined up for us, then," Autumn says with a wink as she snatches up a handful of leaflets. "Nope, nope, nah, no way," she says, quickly scanning each one before dropping it back down and moving along the table.

"Candles!" she snorts, throwing down the leaflet Mom and I had been looking at. "Who'd want to go and visit a candle museum? I mean, *please!*"

I don't say anything as I shuffle some brochures on the table so she can't see the sign-up sheet — and I turn away so she doesn't see my pink cheeks, either.

Suddenly, Autumn's pulling on my arm and jigging up and down like a toddler. "Look at this, Jenni," she says.

It's a brochure for an outdoor adventure park in a village about ten miles away.

"We've got to go!" Autumn says. "Listen to this. They do rock climbing, rappeling, hiking, all sorts of things."

I *knew* she'd try to talk me into something like this. "I don't know," I murmur, playing for time. I mean I know it generally feels great *after* I've done some scary stunt that Autumn's persuaded me is a good idea — but that doesn't mean I'm desperate for the next one. "Rappeling? Rock climbing? Don't those involve heights?" I ask nervously. "I mean — don't you think it could be a bit dangerous?"

"And horseback riding! That's it — we're going!" Autumn bursts out, instantly clicking her teeth and jumping around me, trotting like a horse. "Remember the wooden horses we had in first grade, Jen?"

We'd persuaded our parents to buy us matching hobbyhorses, and we used to trit-trot *everywhere* on them. We pretended we were cowgirls out on the plains hunting for long-lost treasure.

I laugh. "Mm, but like you say, we were in first

grade — and they *were* wooden. No danger of having one of them trample on your feet!"

Autumn stops trotting and turns to look for her mom. She's standing in the middle of the room, her hand on my mom's stomach, smiling as they talk.

"What's going on?" I ask as we join them.

"He kicked," Mom says, beaming.

"He?" Mrs. Leonard asks, raising an eyebrow.

"Well, we don't know for sure," Mom says, "but he feels like a 'he' to me. Feel the kick on those legs, and tell me we haven't got a little soccer player in there!"

I reach out to touch Mom's stomach. A tiny *thump* pushes at my hand. It fills my heart to think there's a little life in there. My baby brother. I can't wait to meet him.

Autumn puts her hand next to mine. *"Awesome!"* she cries. Then she bends down and talks directly to Mom's stomach. "Hey, Jenni's little bro," she says. "Please will you tell Mrs. Green that Jenni and I are going horseback riding?"

"What's that?" her mom asks.

Autumn opens up the brochure. "Horseback riding! We're going tomorrow!" she announces. Autumn doesn't generally do requests. There'd be no point; no one ever says no to her.

"It's tomorrow?" I falter. "But I've just signed up for the trip to . . ." My voice trails off.

"They only do the horseback riding on Sundays," Autumn says, studying the brochure. She started riding lessons this year and thinks it's the best thing ever. I went with her once. I didn't like it all that much, even though I knew I probably should. All girls my age love horses, but I just think they're so . . . well, big! My favorite animals are generally the type you can cuddle without worrying about them standing on your feet and crushing your toes to dust. Cute fluffy ones like puppies and kittens.

"Mom, we can go, can't we?" Autumn persists.

"I don't see why not," her mom answers, looking at the times of the class. "As long as you can get a ride back. We could drop you off, but I'm booked for an aromatherapy massage later on." She turns to my mom. "Can you pick them up?"

"I thought you wanted to go to the candle museum, Jenni," Mom says.

Autumn bursts out laughing as my cheeks heat up.

"I was only doing it for you," I say quickly. "You go

with Craig. I'd rather go horseback riding." And it's true. Suddenly the idea of a candle museum sounds dull to me, too. Even if horseback riding *is* scary, if Autumn's there, I know it'll be more fun than anything else I could be doing.

And, anyway, both of us want to be together as often as possible this week since we're not going to see each other as much once we get home. We go to different middle schools. I go to the local one, while she goes to a magnet school in the next town. Autumn went through months of agony last year, trying to decide where to go. She wanted to be with me, but her dream is to be a famous artist, and everyone said that she should go there, since it's got a great art department. Even I agreed—reluctantly. And apart from missing each other, we're both really happy where we are.

We've always promised each other that it won't change anything between us and that we'll be best friends forever. So far, that seems to be the case. But now that it's the start of another year, I can't help worrying a little. I mean, you never *really* know what's going to happen, do you?

Wouldn't it be great if you did, though? If you

could just have a little glimpse of what the future holds. Just so you'd know. That would be so cool.

"All right, love. Your dad can pick you up," Mom says with a smile. "I'm sure he won't want to be dragged around a boring museum, either."

"Thanks, Mom," I say as Autumn grabs my hand and drags me off.

We pass Dad and Craig coming back in as we leave. "Don't be late," Dad calls after us. "I thought we'd all have a game of Monopoly before Craig's bedtime."

Autumn laughs as she runs outside. "Honestly, Jen. Monopoly? It's nonstop thrills with your family!" Then she pinches me, tickling me till I fall to the ground, laughing hysterically.

Two girls are walking toward us as we chase each other down the path: Christine and Sally. They've been coming here as long as we have. They're about our age, but as different from us as you can get. Both perfect and pretty, with their long blond hair and little pink handbags swinging on their arms. Their pace quickens and their smiles widen when they spot us. Correction: when they spot *Autumn*.

"Hi!" they enthuse in unison, crowding around Autumn and hardly noticing me.

"You want to hang out with us tomorrow?" Christine asks. "I've got a new straightening iron we can try out on each other, or we could go shopping or something." Both girls hold their breath while they wait for Autumn to answer. It's like being best friends with a movie star. Everyone always wants to know Autumn.

"Sorry, we're busy tomorrow," Autumn says lazily. I don't think she even realizes how much everyone craves her company. "Catch up with you later in the week maybe."

The girls try not to show their disappointment. "Cool," Sally says. "See you later."

"Bye, then!" I say pointedly as they turn away.

"Oh, see you, Jenni," Christine calls over her shoulder as an afterthought.

Autumn nudges me once they're out of sight. "Why would I want to hang out with Barbie One and Barbie Two, anyway?" she says.

"Autumn, that's mean!" I say, secretly trying not to smile as we head back down the path, away from the buildings, along the river, and across the long bridge that curves over to a field on the other side.

A bit farther up, the river opens out into its widest

stretch. It's almost a lake, virtually still and shallow. If you watch closely, you can just about see the current slinking forward.

Across the bridge, you can creep around some bushes at the very edge of the lake to a tiny rocky bay hidden around the corner. It's our secret place.

Autumn kicks off her shoes and rolls up her jeans. She splashes into the water, picks up a stone, and skips it across the lake. It bounces six times. "Oh, yes! The stone-skipping champion of the world strikes again!" she whoops.

I edge into the water behind her. It's freezing.

"So what's new?" she asks, scavenging for another flat stone. "Any gossip?"

I laugh. "Gossip? Me? *You're* the one with the exciting life!"

"That's true," she says as she flicks her stone across the lake.

"Hey!" I laugh, kicking water at her.

She bends down to splash me. Laughing and screaming, we chase each other back to the pebbly cove.

Autumn flops down on the stones. "Come on," she says, wiping her feet off with her hands before putting her shoes back on.

"But we just got here."

"Let's go down to the weir and see how full it is."

"It's full. I've seen it."

"Yeah, but not with me, you haven't."

That's how it is with Autumn. As soon as we're doing one thing, she's ready to move on to something else. I follow her as she dances along the path. On the way, I tell her about Craig being sick on the way up and about the book I'm reading, and I point out the leaves that have gone red like they always do. Silly stuff, really, but there's something about sharing things with Autumn that's important. As though nothing's quite real until I have.

It's just starting to get dark when we get back to the condos. The steam train puffs through the woods across the river, letting out its comic little "Toot!" before it disappears under a bridge.

"I wouldn't believe that train was for real if we hadn't actually been on it," Autumn says. "It's like something out of a cartoon."

"Yep. It's definitely real," I say, remembering last year when Craig and Mikey stuck their heads out the window and tooted at the tops of their voices, making an elderly lady jump out of her skin. I thought they'd given her a heart attack.

"It's all so organized here, isn't it?" Autumn continues. "Not like normal life."

"It's certainly nothing like *your* life!" I say with a laugh. "*Nothing's* organized at your house!"

"Don't you ever think it's not like the real world here?" Autumn grabs my arm, her eyes dancing. She hops backward as she talks. "Hey, maybe it's an alternate universe!" Her tone gets higher; her eyes become even more animated. "Or a movie! Maybe we're in one and we don't even know it! Like the one where that guy keeps living the exact same day over and over again."

"Or the one where he finds out that his whole life is really a television show?"

"That's it! Nothing's real up here. It's all just a TV show!" Autumn leaps behind a bush, pretending to hold a camera as she jumps out next to me, filming me as I walk along.

"Yeah, right." I laugh. "Who'd want to make a film of *me*?"

Autumn keeps filming. "Maybe you're not really you but a clone of yourself, and the real you is carrying on a parallel life somewhere else!"

A cold shiver flashes up my back and neck. What if something like that was really possible? Then I laugh. "You've been reading too much science fiction," I say.

Autumn pretends to throw the camera over her shoulder. "You're right," she says, laughing. "Did I tell you about the book I'm reading now?"

And the conversation's forgotten as she recounts the story of a boy who lives his whole life not knowing that he's a clone of his dead brother. Creepy.

We've reached her building.

"You coming in?"

"I'd better get back," I say. "Dad'll start looking if I'm not in soon."

"See you tomorrow, then," Autumn calls as she pushes the big glass door open. "Enjoy Monopoly!" She blows me an elaborate kiss and waves as I leave.

A second later, I hear a loud clanking noise from inside, like something falling. Autumn!

I run into the foyer. It's all marble and water features. Autumn's building is different from the others: fancier and older. The elevator's on one side, next to another, older elevator that doesn't work, and there's a big arch leading to the first-floor hallway opposite. An ornate mirror hangs on the wall across from the entrance, in between a couple of other doors. One of them is open.

"Hello?" I call. "Autumn?"

No answer. She's gone; there's no one around, and there's nothing out of place, either. I turn to leave, but just as I'm about to open the door, I look back to see someone coming out of the old elevator. He's got a pile of logs in his arms, so high I can't see his face, and an ax gripped under his elbow. Must be the caretaker.

But then I notice his hair over the top of the logs. It's Mr. Barraclough! What's he doing here? I mean, I know he does do a few odd jobs around the place — doesn't mind "rolling up his sleeves," as he puts it — but why is he taking the logs out of the elevator?

It's one of those really old-fashioned ones with a big metal gate that you have to pull across. It's never worked, as far as I know, and it's just used as a storage space. The new elevator next to it works fine, so I don't think anyone's ever bothered to try to get it working.

"Hi," I say from the doorway. As he glances up at me, a couple of logs fall from his arms.

"Drat," he mutters, bending to pick them up, but dropping more in the process.

"Can I help?" I ask, hurrying to pick the logs up for him.

"Thanks." He points to the open door. "I'm transferring all these things into that closet."

"Why are you doing that?" I ask, stacking the logs on a shelf in the closet.

Mr. Barraclough shakes his head slowly as he returns to the old elevator for another stash. "Good question," he says, his voice cracking slightly. Almost in a whisper, he adds, "Trying to get the old thing working, like the silly fool that I am." He gets a wrench out of his pocket and waves it at me. "Broken wires, you see. Thought I'd have a go at fixing them. Silly," he says with a laugh. "But you never know. It just might have . . ." His voice fades away. He doesn't look at me as he speaks. It doesn't even feel as though he's talking to me.

He stands there, looking down at his feet, till I start to feel awkward. Has he lost his mind? He's not making the slightest bit of sense.

"Um, I'd better be . . . um . . ." I point to the entrance, my voice trailing away.

Mr. Barraclough suddenly seems to remember I'm there. "Yes, of course." He fixes a quick smile in my direction. "Sorry. Ignore me—silly old fool. Thanks for your help. Off you go, now."

"Right. Bye," I say before I scurry away, wondering if perhaps he'd had a tad too much champagne at the welcome meeting. It was as though he'd slipped off into another world—sort of like he did at the meeting, too.

And I don't know if it's because of the sci-fi story or all those things Autumn was talking about, but the thought suddenly fires up my imagination. What if we *could* slip into another world, just by thinking about it? What if we could travel into a different dimension whenever we wanted, travel through space and time with a click of the fingers?

For a second, the idea grips me so hard, it makes my whole body twitch and prickle, and I can't wait to share it with Autumn. But when I try to imagine putting it into words, the idea seems to dissolve and slip away from me, and a moment later, I can't recapture it at all.

As I walk back to our condo, I laugh at myself. That's what hanging out with Autumn does to you—makes you start believing in impossible things. I mean, fantasy worlds and different dimensions—as if!

3

Mom pokes her head around the door.

"Jenni, are you going to have some breakfast?"

"I'll be out in a minute," I groan. She takes this as an invitation to come in and open the curtains. A chink of bright light cuts across the room. *"Mom!"* I pull the covers farther over my head.

"Come on. We want to figure out our plans for the day," she says as she closes the door behind her.

I don't normally sleep in. It's this place. It always takes me hours to get to sleep on the first night. You can hear the river running outside the window. At home, we live near railroad tracks. I can quite happily sleep through cargo trains going past three times a night, but a river? Too noisy.

Once I do get to sleep, it always seems much deeper here. I have vivid technicolor dreams, and then I wake up in a daze and can't drag myself out of bed.

I reach for my diary. I like to write in the mornings, right after I wake up. When I finally make it into the living room, it's nearly eleven o'clock. Craig's sitting cross-legged on the floor about four inches away from the television, watching a cartoon. Mom's on the sofa with the Sunday newspaper spread out around her. Dad's doing the dishes.

"Afternoon," Dad says without looking up.

"Sorry, couldn't wake up," I say as I pour some cereal into a bowl. "Happy anniversary," I add, handing Mom a card.

"Oh, sweetheart, that's nice of you," she says, smiling. Dad dries his hands and joins her on the sofa so they can open the card together. It's got two teddy bears on it, sitting in a boat.

"Thanks, sweet pea," Dad says with a wink before going back to the dishes.

"So, shall we plan our day, now that we're all here?" Mom asks. "We've got the restaurant booked for tonight, haven't we, Tom?"

Dad nods. Their anniversary dinner. They always go to this fancy restaurant to celebrate. Usually, someone babysits me and Craig, but Mom insists we all go this year. She wants it to be a celebration of the family, she says, not just her and Dad. I guess with the little one on the way, this is one of the last times that going out as a family will mean just the four of us.

"I'm going horseback riding this afternoon, remember," I call from the table as I shovel cereal into my mouth.

"And I'm playing squash," Dad calls from the sink.

"What time?" Mom asks.

"Four fifteen, why?"

Mom turns to me. "What time does horseback riding finish, Jenni?"

"Four thirty."

"Well, that's it, then," she says to Dad. "You'll have to cancel squash."

"What? How d'you work that out?"

"I told Autumn's parents we'd pick up the girls. They're dropping them off; it's only fair."

"Oh, no! Can't you pick them up?"

"I signed up for the candle museum tour with Craig."

"Well, I signed up for squash," Dad says. He dries his hands on a dish towel and comes back to the sofa to snuggle up with Mom. He tickles her cheek and kisses her neck. "I think you might even find that I signed up for squash first," he says. "Although if it's too much for you . . ."

Mom slaps his hand away from her cheek. "I don't really know why you bother with squash. It's not as though you're any good at it," she says, laughing.

"Hey!" He tickles her harder, till Mom begs him to stop.

"OK, OK, I'll do it!" she screeches eventually.

Dad turns serious. "Are you sure? I mean, you're definitely up to it?"

"I'm only pregnant; I'm not incapacitated," she says. "It's fine. I'll take Craig to the museum in the car, and then we won't have to wait for the bus back."

"Look, neither of you needs to cancel anything," I say. "We *can* get a bus, you know."

"No, you can't," Dad says. "Not on your own."

"Dad, I'm twelve. I'm not a baby."

"I know, sweet pea, but it's a long way, and you've never been before. We don't even know if there *is* a bus."

"I'll pick you up. It's fine, honestly," Mom says.

I rinse my bowl. Why do they always have to treat me like a little kid? I suddenly feel crowded and claustrophobic. "I'm going to see Autumn."

"Do you need to spend *every* minute with Autumn?" Dad asks. "You're seeing her this afternoon." He gets up off the sofa to follow me out of the room. "I had actually wondered if we might all go for a walk this morning." He nearly trips over Craig, still motionless on the floor, his jaw open, eyes fixed on cartoon aliens. "Craig, you've watched enough of that," Dad says. "Turn it off now."

"It's just getting to a good part," Craig whines.

"I said *off*." Dad walks over to the TV and switches it off.

Craig instantly breaks into a wail. He sounds like an air-raid siren.

"I'm outta here," I say, heading for the door. I pause. "Is that OK? Maybe we can have a walk later?"

Dad lets out a breath. "Never mind. I'll take Craig, and your mom can rest."

"Do I have to?" Craig bleats. "Can't I go with Jenni?"

"No, you can't," I say. The last thing I want right now is my little brother at my heels.

"I'll be back in a bit," I add, and head over to Autumn's building.

43

I stand in Autumn's foyer, waiting for the elevator, feeling frustrated and fed up. It isn't coming. I've pressed the button, but nothing's happening. The stairs are on the other side of the building, so I hardly ever use them. A young couple passes me, holding hands and smiling into each other's eyes as they leave the building. They don't even notice me. I bet they're here on their honeymoon.

I'll have to use the stairs. I can't wait to talk to Autumn. She's the only person who understands me. I mean my family's all right, as families go. But it's still a family, isn't it? Still parents who treat you like you're a little kid and don't trust you to do anything yourself.

What's the matter with the elevator?

I'll just have to use the stairs, I guess. Just as I'm thinking this, I pass the old elevator, the one that's never worked. I bang my fist on its door. "Stupid elevator," I say.

And then I hear something. A whirring noise, and a thumping and banging from inside the elevator. Then a tapping noise, getting louder, coming nearer! I stand back. Finally — *CLANK!* Mr. Barraclough must have fixed the elevator after all!

I pull the heavy metal door open. Behind it, there's

another door, also metal, with concertina brass bars ridged across it, like a gate.

I pull it open and go into the elevator. It's so old and run-down, I don't believe for a minute it could work. What if I get inside and it plummets down for miles, taking me with it?

I laugh at myself. Sometimes my imagination really does work overtime. It's not going to plummet anywhere. Besides, it's not as if the other one looks like it's coming—and I've always found this elevator fascinating.

There are four black buttons on the wall: *4, 3, 2,* and *1.* Underneath the buttons, a piece of plywood is nailed to the wall; above them there's a bright-red button with ALARM written beside it. Above that, a notice says, "Please close both doors as you exit the elevator. Thank you."

I pull the outer door closed, then slide the gate across, shutting out the light except for a tiny sliver poking through the grated window in the door.

I've never been in an old-fashioned elevator like this before. It makes me feel like I'm in an old spy movie. Maybe Autumn and I could invent a story about it. I make a mental note to add it to my list of things I want to talk to her about.

And then I press the button for the second floor.

For a moment, nothing happens. I wait in the gloom as a tiny ball of panic starts to uncurl in my stomach. Why didn't I just take the stairs?

And then it moves. Clunking into action, it rattles upward, scraping and rumbling to the next floor. Then, with a giant *THUD* that makes my teeth rattle, it jumps to a halt.

I step out and shut the doors behind me.

Autumn's condo is right at the end of the hallway. I knock our special rap on the door. *Tap-tappity-tap-tap,* pause, *tap-tap.*

Nothing.

I knock again and then peer over the railing to the parking lot. Three cars down there, but not Autumn's. You don't easily miss a bright-red Porsche. Where are they? I bang heavily on the door one last time before giving up and turning away.

I run down the stairs this time and out to the front of the building. For a second, I think I hear Autumn's voice and I stop and listen, but I don't hear it again. Maybe they've gone out for the morning.

I try our spot by the lake, but someone else is there. A group of young kids and two sets of parents. That's *our* place! But I don't stop to argue with them. It's not as if there's a law against other people going there.

The shore looks bigger than yesterday. It seems to reach even farther back, a whole beach of gray-and-white stones.

Maybe Autumn's at the weir. I run down there and call her name. Two teenage boys seem to be trying to cross the weir. They must be nuts! It's so high at the moment, they're bound to kill themselves. I edge toward them. That's when I see something *really* odd. The weir — it's not rushing and gushing over the top like Niagara Falls anymore. It's more like a little stream, a slow, shallow dribble over the long wall that stretches across the river.

How did that happen? I suppose it hasn't rained overnight. Is that all it takes — one night of no rain?

On the way back to our condo, I have a quick look in the rec center. Maybe Autumn and her family have gone for a swim, especially since we didn't have any plans till this afternoon. No one in that family ever sits down for longer than half a minute.

But they're not there. They must have gone for a walk or something.

Without telling me?

I decide to try their condo one last time. My frustration seems to have given me energy, so I wander around to the other side of their building, run up the stairs, and march down the corridor to their condo.

Tap-tappity-tap-tap. Tap-tap.

Come on, Autumn. Be in. I don't want to have to go home.

There's a noise behind the door. "Who is it?" a voice calls. A strange voice. Pleasant and sweet, it reminds me of a birdcall—but it's not the voice of anyone in Autumn's family.

"It's me," I call back, slightly uncertainly. "Jenni."

"Jenni who?" the voice sings back to me.

"Jenni! Um . . . do you want to let me in?" I ask, even more uncertainly. Whose voice *is* that?

The door opens. A woman I've never seen in my life is holding on to the doorknob. Probably in her fifties, she's got graying hair tied back in a ponytail, and she's wearing a long, floaty red dress and gold flip-flops. She smiles at me. "Can I help you, dear?" she asks.

"Who are you?" I gasp, stepping back to check the door. Number 210. Autumn's condo.

"Who are *you*?" the woman retorts.

"Autumn's friend."

"Autumn's friend? What does that mean?"

"My friend's parents own this condo."

"I'm afraid they don't. This is my condo. You must have made a mistake, dear. Sorry." She smiles kindly at me and moves to close the door.

"Wait!" The woman pauses, the door open just wide enough so I can see her eyes. "Have you definitely got the right week?" I ask. "They own it the last week of August. Are you just leaving?" My questions don't make sense, even to me. She can't be leaving! They've already arrived. They got here last night. "Are you staying with them?" I ask, searching my memory to work out who she could be. I've met Autumn's grandma. It's not her. A friend of the family?

"I've told you, dear," the woman says. "This is my condo, my week. I arrived yesterday; I don't know anything about your friend." She smiles again, slightly more woodenly this time. "As I said, I'm ever so sorry I can't help you. Now, if you don't mind, I'll get back to my needlepoint. Is there anything else?"

"I . . ."

The woman waits a bit longer.

"Well, all right, then," she says. "I'll be going. Sorry again, dear. Hope you find your friend." And with that, she closes the door.

I stare at the number: 210. I trace each digit with my fingers. Two, one, zero. It *is* their condo. Am I going crazy?

Finally, I turn to go home, walking blindly down the hallway, completely shaken. The old elevator is standing open, waiting for me. I walk into it in a daze, close the outer door, pull the metal gate closed, and hit the button for the first floor. All the way home, I go over what just happened, arguing and reasoning with myself to try to make sense of it. I must have gotten the wrong condo. Maybe they changed it without telling me. They *must* have. Or I went to the wrong floor by mistake.

By the time I get back to our condo, I've just about managed to convince myself that the whole thing was my own stupid mistake. Nothing to worry about at all. I'm not losing my mind. There'll be a simple explanation. There's got to be.

4

Dad's hunched over the living-room table, writing. "Autumn's been looking for you," he says without glancing up.

"What? She's been here?"

"You just missed her. Left five minutes ago. Maybe ten. Said she'd been looking all over for you. Listen, what d'you think of this? 'The river raced ruggedly down the hill, falling over itself as though it was in a hurry.'" He looks up. "It's the opening of my novel."

"It's great, Dad. I thought you'd already begun your novel."

Dad leans back over his notebook. "Starting a new one. I just got a fresh idea. It's this place—it inspires me. We should come here more often."

I get some orange juice from the fridge. "Did Autumn say where she was going?"

"Back to their condo."

"Back to their condo?"

"That's what I said."

"And she left ten minutes ago?" I sip my juice.

"Correct."

"Dad, have they swapped their condo?"

"Good grief, Jen, what's with the Spanish Inquisition? Not that I know of. Why don't you ask her when she comes by? She said she'd come back in a bit."

Of course. I'll just ask her. There'll be a simple explanation. "Where's Mom?" I ask.

"Taken Craig for a swim."

"Are they — ?"

"Look, Jenni, I'm just trying to do some work. No offense, but do you mind . . . ?"

I shake my head as I wash my glass out in the sink. Let him convince himself he's writing an internationally best-selling blockbuster.

Something catches my eye outside the window and I look up. Autumn. At last! I run to the door to let her in.

"Where've you *been?*" we squeal in unison before I grab her arm and drag her inside.

"Hi, Mr. Green," she calls through the door. Dad waves a hand absentmindedly in reply. We go upstairs to my room, and I close the door behind us. "I couldn't find you anywhere—it was like you'd disappeared into thin air!" Autumn says.

"I know! What on earth happened?"

"Spooky!" she says, laughing and pretending to play creepy music on a piano in midair.

"I know. Completely bizarre. I couldn't make any sense of it at first, but I've realized I must have just made a mistake with your condo."

"My condo?"

"Yeah. When did you change it?"

"Change what?" Autumn tilts her head at me, waiting for me to explain.

"The . . . the . . . your . . . condo?" I falter.

"We haven't changed it," Autumn says, screwing up her nose at me.

"And your car," I add, feeling like an idiot. "It wasn't there."

"Of course it was, you dope!" Autumn says. Then she half covers her eyes and walks around the room banging into things. "You must have had blinders on."

She walks into the side of the bed and does this really over-the-top fall onto it, making me laugh. She's right — it was obviously just me being stupid. I force it out of my mind and convince myself that there'll be an explanation.

"Hey, I've got a present for you," she says, sitting up and pulling something out of her pocket. "Close your eyes and hold out your hand."

I do as she says, and she places something on my palm. I close my hand around it.

"Open your eyes!"

It's a necklace made from some pebbles with wire mesh holding them in place. It's lovely and unusual: exactly the kind of thing Autumn does — and the kind of thing that makes her so amazing.

"I made it last night," she says, grinning broadly. "They're from our place. It's a friendship necklace."

I sit down next to her and hug her. "I love it. Thank you." Autumn watches me as I tie it around my neck.

"You're welcome," she says, jumping off the bed. "So — tell me more about the weird stuff. Maybe you weren't walking around with blinders on after all. Maybe our car was abducted by aliens."

"What would aliens want with a bright-red Porsche?" I ask, laughing.

"Maybe they're going to turn it into a spaceship and

use it for races between their planet and ours." She goes over to the French door and opens it up. The river roars loudly past.

"Or maybe they come from a planet where everything's red," I say. "Bit by bit, they're going to steal all the red things from our planet."

Autumn jumps up and down and claps her hands. "Yeah, that's it!" she exclaims. "Yay — no more beets!"

"No more tomatoes!"

"Oh." Autumn slumps back onto the bed, her smile gone.

"What is it?" I ask.

"No more ketchup," she says glumly. An instant later, she brightens up again. "Oh, well — we'll just have to hope it's not the aliens at all and that it was just you not noticing our car."

I pause for a moment, remembering all the other things that were different. "No, it was more than that," I say tentatively.

"Like what?" Autumn looks intensely into my eyes. Then she glances around the room. She picks up one of my sneakers and shoves it under the bed. "Lost your shoes as well, did you?" Then she puts on a fake mysterious voice. "Hey," she says, pointing at the floor,

"I'm sure there was a shoe down there before. It's such a mystery!"

I laugh and shove her onto the bed. "No, really. It was *definitely* more than that," I say seriously. "Where were you, anyway?"

Autumn shrugs. "The lake, the weir, at home, looking for you."

All the same places I'd been. How could we have missed each other at every place?

"Autumn."

She's reaching under the bed, fiddling with the arm of one of Craig's discarded robots. It comes off in her hand. "Uh-huh?"

"It was strange. I don't know how to explain it."

"Ooh, goody!" Autumn puts down the robot's arm and crosses her legs. "Come on, then. Tell me more."

"Only if you promise not to make fun of me."

Autumn pulls an ultra-serious face. "I promise," she says solemnly.

So I tell her about going to her condo and about the woman in the floaty dress and how I couldn't see Autumn or her family anywhere.

"Cool!" she says. "I must have turned invisible!"

"I'm being serious!"

"*I'm* being serious. What other explanation is there?"

"Autumn, you seriously think you've become invisible?"

"Why not? If you can clone people and you can find out your whole life is a TV show, what makes you so convinced you can't become invisible?"

"Autumn, those were stories!"

"Who says this isn't?"

I pick up some LEGOs from the floor and throw them onto Craig's bed. Why does he have to make such a mess? "How come my dad could see you, then?" I ask. "And what about the woman in the condo? And where was your car?"

"I said. It was there all morning," Autumn says. "You did go to the right place, didn't you?"

"Building C, number 210. End condo, second floor."

"Yep, that's us." Autumn jumps off the bed and bounds over to the window again. It's started raining, fat splodges squashing lazily against the glass. She pulls the French door closed and stands looking out. "OK, I can't explain that," she says finally.

"I must have gotten it wrong," I say. "Had a brain drain. I did. I went to the wrong condo — I'm sure of it now." I don't know who I'm more determined to convince — Autumn or myself. Autumn seems happy

57

enough with my conclusion — even if I'm not so sure. Seeing as I don't have a better explanation, I decide to ignore the bit of my brain that's silently trying to argue against my words.

"Well, that's that, then," Autumn says, turning around. "And I suppose we probably just kept missing each other. I guess I didn't turn invisible after all."

"I guess."

"Shame."

"Yeah."

The front door bangs. "We're home!" Mom calls.

Autumn jumps off the bed and glances at her watch. "I need to go home for lunch. Come by at two, OK?"

"OK."

Autumn pokes her head into the living room as we pass. "Hi, Mrs. Green."

"Hi, Autumn," Mom replies as she hangs Craig's towel over the radiator.

"Did you swim?" I ask.

Mom smiles and pats her stomach. "With this? It'd be like a blue whale getting in the pool!"

"We saw workmen with a digger and they talked to us, and Mom said I can go back and watch them work tomorrow, didn't you, Mom?" Craig tells us eagerly.

Mom ruffles his wet hair. "Yes, darling."

"I'll see you later?" Autumn says, glancing at the clock. "I gotta go."

I walk her to the door. "See ya!" she says. And with that, she dances down the sidewalk, pausing just before she goes out of sight to wave and blow me her usual flamboyant kiss. "We're leaving at two on the dot," she calls. "Don't be late."

"I won't."

"Condo 210!"

"Yes, don't worry. I'll come to the right place this time." I force a laugh.

Once she's out of sight, I turn back to go inside, closing the door behind me.

"Jenni, set the table for your mom," Dad says. He's still sitting at the table.

"You'll have to move, then."

"In a minute. Can't stop when it's flowing. You've heard of the person from Porlock, haven't you?"

"Yes, Dad. We've all heard of the person from Porlock."

He tells us this story about once a week. Some guy was writing a poem or something, and he was interrupted by someone at the door: the person from Porlock. And that was the end of that. His inspiration was broken, and the poem was never completed. It would have been a brilliant work of genius, and he never finished it. Great story. It's basically Dad's way of getting out of doing anything around the house.

"OK, lunch." Mom brings a tray of sandwiches to the table as I get the plates.

Dad leans across to kiss her. She touches the back of his head, holding him close to her. When they move apart, they smile at each other. He kisses her cheek. "Fifteen years. Who'd have thought it, Mrs. Green?" Dad says.

Mom smiles and leans down to rest her head on his shoulder. Then Dad gets up to clear away his note-books. "Come on, Craig." Craig's in front of the TV again. "Lunch."

Normality. Thank goodness for that. For a moment, I forget all about the weird things and almost manage to convince myself that they didn't happen. Life is calm and peaceful again, as it should be. As it always is. The normal, predictable Green family household — just how we like it.

As I go into Autumn's building, the old elevator is standing open. I'm sure I closed it behind me. It's as though it saw me coming and opened especially for me.

The other one doesn't come when I call it, so I step inside the old one and go up to the second floor. With the slightest jitter in my stomach, I stand outside number 210, staring at the door. *Definitely* Autumn's condo! I straighten my clothes. My top feels tight. Maybe I shouldn't have had a whole bag of potato chips with my lunch.

I knock on the door.

"Who is it?"

Oh, no! It's her again! But it *can't* be! This is the right place; I checked and double-checked. What is going *on*?

The door opens a fraction.

"I'm sorry. I . . ."

The woman stares blankly at me for a split second and then registers recognition. "You again," she says quietly. "What do you want with me now?" She's not as friendly as last time. Her voice has an edge to it that could just be irritation but almost sounds scared.

"I'm just looking for Autumn," I say.

"What do you mean, looking for autumn? How do you lose a season?"

As she says this, her face suddenly drains of all color. She pushes the door farther closed — her eyes big and shocked against her suddenly gray face. When

61

she talks again, it's as though she's looking straight through me and talking to a ghost.

"You're trying to make a fool of me, aren't you?" she says. "You know! But how? It's impossible. No one knows—no one *ever* knew. Only me. Always lost."

What's she talking about? "I—I don't know what you mean," I say, trying to sound as reasonable and unthreatening as I possibly can. "I'm not trying to do anything bad. I just want to find Autumn. We're going out in a minute."

The woman has stopped staring beyond me and seems to have remembered I'm here. "Look." She reaches a thin arm through the crack and points to the numbers on the door. "My condo—210. My week. How many times do you need to be told?"

I can feel my eyes sting. "I don't know," I say. "I don't *know* how many times I need to be told. All I know is that it doesn't make sense!"

The woman stares at me, holding my gaze for so long that I want to turn away, but the link between us feels so strong, it's like a magnet and I can't move a muscle. "What doesn't make sense?" she asks eventually.

"This is Autumn's condo. I'm sure it is. They've been here for the last three years. I saw her an hour ago!"

She stares a bit longer, as though she's trying to

read my mind. That's when I realize — it's a joke! She's going to tell me, any second. It's Autumn messing with me. I should have known she'd do something like this. She loves pranks!

"This is a joke, isn't it?" I say, feeling my body relax with relief as I smile at her.

"I thought as much," the woman says. "Look, I don't know where you got your facts, but it's not funny."

"No —" I try to backtrack. "I mean — I thought you were playing a joke on me."

The woman lets out a harsh laugh. "*Me* playing a joke on *you*?" she snaps. Then she shakes her head. "You need to go now," she says. "Or I'm calling the police."

And with that, she closes the door.

I try knocking again.

"I mean it," she shouts through the door, her voice shaking. "I'll phone them. You'll be in trouble."

I can't stay here; things are just going from bad to worse. I check my watch. Past two o'clock. They're going to leave without me.

A man I vaguely recognize is going into a condo at the end of the hallway. I think he's a friend of Mr. Leonard's.

"Excuse me!" I call. He turns around, and I run to catch up with him. "I'm looking for Autumn," I say.

"Autumn?"

"The Leonards, you know. Autumn and Mikey and their parents. They have a condo in this building. Don't you know her dad?"

"Well, yes. I do. But . . ." The man gives me a really weird look. As though I'm stupid and shouldn't be allowed to wander around on my own. He fiddles with the strap of his bag and slings it over his shoulder.

"Have you seen them?" I ask, a little impatiently. Any second now, I'm going to be too late. They've probably gone without me already. It's nearly quarter past two.

"Well, I haven't seen them up here," he says. "Have you tried their condo?"

"I've just *been* there!" I cry, frustration burning into my throat. "They're not there. There's just this woman I've never seen before. Didn't you just see me in the hallway?"

"How could I have seen you?" He laughs. "I haven't been downstairs."

"Huh? But we were there a second ago. Just over there." I point down the hallway. Why is everyone talking in riddles to me today? What's going *on* here?

The man takes his bag off his shoulder and puts

it down. He draws in a breath, then kind of puffs his cheeks out and looks away.

"What is it?" I ask.

"Have you seen the family recently?" His face is grim.

"Yes!" I scream. "I was with Autumn an hour ago, and we're supposed to be going out together. I've probably missed them now. Where are they? Do you know?"

"Listen. Why don't you just try their condo again?"

"But I've just been there! I keep telling you! No one's come or gone since we've been standing here!"

"How do you know?"

"Because we'd have seen them!" What is this man's *problem*? "Look, thanks for your help," I say, walking away. "I'm sure I'll find her."

"It's 114," he says.

I turn around. "What?"

"That's their condo, 114. First floor."

"What are you talking about?" I ask, shaking my head. "That's not their condo. It's 210."

"Just try it," he says. He shakes his head as he pushes his door open and steps inside. "I can't believe you didn't know about them changing their condo. She's your friend, isn't she?" he adds before closing the door behind him.

Like everything else, his words make no sense to me, so I try not to dwell on them.

I decide to take the stairs now that I'm at this end of the hallway. I might as well go home. They're bound to have left without me. The man obviously doesn't know what he's talking about. The Leonards always have this condo — he must have been thinking of a different family

I check the parking lot on the way out. There's no sign of a gleaming, sparkling Porsche, just a couple of old cars that they wouldn't be seen dead in! I knew it. It's nearly twenty past two. They've gone without me.

But as I leave the parking lot, I glance at the first floor and notice that the doors have changed color! They used to be brown; now they're white. But that's impossible. They couldn't have painted them over-night, could they?

I glance at the number on the last one: 114. The one that man said was Autumn's.

But he didn't know what he was talking about, did he? He must have thought I meant someone else.

Still, there's nothing else to do if I've missed them, so I might as well give it a try.

I walk up to condo 114 and take a deep breath. For some reason, a flutter of nerves twirls around in my stomach. *Don't be silly,* I say to myself. *What is there to be nervous about?*

Then I reach up and knock on the door.

5

Jenni. Am I pleased to see you!"

Autumn takes my hand and pulls me into the hallway.

At least, I *think* it's Autumn.

I mean, of course it's her, but she looks so different! Her hair that's always completely crazy and full of life is lank and greasy. It's about six inches longer than it was this morning and hangs down the sides of her face like a damp mop.

Her eyes are black and ringed. She's wearing baggy jeans and a T-shirt that was possibly white at some point but is now a very unattractive gray—and I think it has a stain on it.

"Autumn?" I say tentatively. "Are you . . . OK?"

She stops in the hallway. "What d'you mean?"

"I — your —" What can I say? *You look dreadful, and when was the last time you washed you hair or your clothes?* I don't think so.

"Oh, you mean about being here?" she says.

Being here? *Being where?*

"Yeah, it's weird," she goes on. "It's really hard. To be honest, I'm not sure why we came. Mom was insistent, though. Last place we had a family vacation — she wanted to mark it, you know? Not that you could call it a vacation. More like torture. Come on, let's go in and sit down."

As I follow Autumn into the living room of this strange condo, I try to make sense of what she's just said — but fail badly. Out of all of it, the part that puzzles me the most is the last bit. *Sit down?* When did Autumn ever voluntarily sit down?

We go into the living room, and I follow Autumn to the sofas at the back of the room, looking around at this strange place.

Their normal condo is one of the biggest units in the whole complex. It's light and sunny with views for miles across the surrounding forest and hills; the windows are always open, and they always have music on. Mrs. Leonard likes world music with loads of drumming, and Mr. Leonard likes jazz. They always argue about what to put on — but there's always something.

This condo is small and still. The windows are closed. I'm struggling to breathe regularly. I don't know if it's because I'm starting to panic or because this place feels so closed and claustrophobic that there isn't enough oxygen for us both in here. And it's deathly quiet.

"Where is everyone?" I ask.

"Dad's at the bar in town — of course. Mom hasn't come out of her room for about an hour. I think she's asleep," she says.

"What about Mikey?"

Autumn shoots me a look of — what? Anger? Shock? Pain? All three of them, I think. She stares at me without speaking, till I feel my cheeks turn to balls of fire.

"What?" I ask.

"Jenni, that's not funny," she says quietly.

"I wasn't trying to — " I begin, but I stop myself. *Just don't say anything,* I tell myself. *Concentrate on trying to breathe, and it'll make sense in a minute.*

"Do you want to watch a movie?" Autumn asks, getting up to riffle through the collection of DVDs in a drawer by the TV. "We'll need to stay in so we're here when Mom gets up."

Watch a movie? Autumn never, and I mean *never,* suggests watching TV — not when there's a day to be explored and bounced around in. And, anyway —

"Are we not going, then?" I ask.

"Going where?" Autumn says without turning around. She's reading the back of one of the DVDs. "This looks good," she says. "Listen . . ."

"Horseback riding," I say.

Autumn drops the DVD on the floor and turns to look at me. Her face has turned a pale shade of gray; her eyes look like black wells, buried deep in a long, tired face. *"What?"* she says.

"Horseback riding?" I repeat, more uncertainly this time. I can hear the quiver in my voice — what am I so scared of? What is *happening* here? "You said two o'clock."

Autumn slowly shakes her head. "I can't believe you're saying this, Jenni."

"I'm — I thought we were going horseback riding," I stammer, trying to hold on to the one thing I know for sure is meant to be happening. "You persuaded me," I continue. "I didn't want to go, but you insisted, and I knew it'd be fun — if I was there with you. So we were going. At two o'clock . . ." My voice trails off and disappears into the silence of the living room, swallowed up and dying away to nothing.

Autumn rubs her eyes. "I can't handle this. We've all been through enough. It wasn't an easy decision for us to come here, you know. Please don't make it worse with silly games."

I haven't got the first idea what she's talking about. All I know is I'm starting to feel like I can't breathe.

I stumble to my feet.

"Where are you going?" Autumn asks.

"I — I don't know," I say. It seems to be my answer to everything right now — but I haven't got a better one.

"Jenni, I'm sorry," Autumn says. "Don't go. Come on, let's just hang out and try to be normal for a change. It's so long since we've seen each other!"

"What? We're always together!"

Autumn just gives me another of those looks, and I think she's about to answer, when a weak voice calls her name from one of the other rooms.

"Oh, well, time's up, I guess," Autumn says, putting the DVD back in the drawer and getting up. "Come on."

I want to say, *Come on where?* but I don't even trust

myself to speak any more, so I just follow her into the back bedroom.

The first thing I notice is how dark it is. The curtains are closed, and there's a stale smell in the air. Not totally unpleasant, just not fresh and alive. And not how it normally smells when you're anywhere near Autumn's family. Apart from her mom's expensive perfume, their house always smells of paint or incense — and fresh air. Whatever the time of year, the house always feels so *alive*.

It feels anything but alive now.

There's a suitcase on the floor that no one's bothered to unpack yet. The dark silence makes even the air feel heavy. There's a really horrible feeling crawling up through my body, which — like everything else in here — I can't explain.

Then I notice Autumn's mom.

She looks small and lost, sitting propped up on a chair in the corner. Her hair's loose and untidy. It often is, but this is different. It normally has that "just got out of bed" look that takes hours to create. This time she clearly *has* just gotten out of bed. And she's wearing a baggy sweat suit. She never wears anything except either designer outfits or trendy jeans and paint-spattered smocks. Her eyes are dark.

"Mrs. Leonard, I . . ." *I what exactly? I think maybe I'm losing my mind, and I wonder if you can help me find it?*

She turns her face in my direction, and I notice there's a thin squiggly black line snaking down each cheek.

"Mrs. Leonard! What's wrong?" I say.

"What's *wrong*?" she replies. "What's *wrong,* Jenni?" Then she turns away again and doesn't say any more.

Then I realize — that's what must have happened. We're not going horseback riding because Mrs. Leonard is sick and can't take us.

I turn to Autumn. "You know, I could ask my mom if she could take us if you like," I say. "I don't think they'll have left for the candle museum yet."

Autumn glares at me. "What are you talking about, Jenni?"

Mrs. Leonard drags a hand through her hair — or tries to, anyway. It snags on a knot. "Take you where?" she asks.

"Nowhere," Autumn says quickly. I open my mouth but shut it again without saying anything.

In a lower voice, Autumn says, "Jenni, please. You're going to upset Mom. I want to see if we can get her out of the bedroom today. Just think about what you're saying."

I don't know *what* to think about what I'm saying, or what to think about what *she's* saying, either. So I mutter, "OK," and decide not to say anything else.

Autumn smiles at me. "Thanks, Jenni. You've always been a good friend. I'm glad I've had you to talk to about everything that's happened this year." Then, before I can even begin to ask what she means, she goes over to the window and starts to open the curtains. "OK, come on now, Mom," she says in a bright tone of voice that sounds false — as though she's talking to a patient in a hospital, not her normal *naturally* bright voice. "Let's get you up, shall we?"

She pulls on the first curtain, and her mom turns away. "Close it," her mom says firmly. "Don't push me, Autumn. I'm not ready."

Autumn drops the curtain and takes a sharp breath. "OK," she says calmly. "Do you want a cup of tea, then?"

Mrs. Leonard nods. "Thank you," she says in a whisper. "You're good girls, both of you."

I follow Autumn into the kitchen. This has gone far enough. I need to know what's going on.

"Autumn," I say.

"Mm-hmm?" she says as she fills the kettle at the sink.

"Listen to me."

"I'm listening."

"Autumn, look at me," I say.

Autumn flicks the kettle on. "What?" she says, turning around to look at me. Her face is so pale, her eyes so tired and big and — sad.

"Autumn, what's happened?" I ask.

"What d'you mean?"

"I mean everything! Your mom, you, even the condo. It's all different!"

Autumn looks around the condo. "I know," she says. "Pretty awful, isn't it? It's the best we can do at the moment, since we don't have as much money anymore. I didn't want to come at all, but Mom and Dad thought it would help, you know, come to terms with it."

"Autumn — stop!" I shout, slamming my hands over my ears. I can't listen to this any longer. I can't cope with hearing all these things that don't make sense anymore.

Autumn takes a step toward me. "Jenni, what is it?" she asks, her voice full of concern. "Are you OK? Has something happened to you?"

I shake my head. "Has something happened to *me?*" I say numbly. I don't know what else to say. I take a big breath and let it out in a long whistle as I try to find the words.

"Autumn — my head is bursting with so many questions, I think it's going to explode."

"What questions? Tell me. You can still ask me anything, you know. You don't need to stop yourself just because of all this. I'm still your best friend."

I nod. OK. Questions. Where to start?

"Where's your dad?" I ask eventually.

Autumn laughs drily. "Like I said, at the bar, I presume," she says. "Where else would he be?"

Her answer makes about as much sense as everything else. Autumn's parents are hardly ever apart, and they don't generally drink anything except champagne or cocktails. Mr. Leonard certainly isn't the type to hang out in the local bar all day.

"So where's Mikey?" I ask.

Autumn's jaw falls open. "Why are you asking me that?" she says.

I stare back at her. "I just thought . . . he — he's not here. Is he in his room?"

Autumn stares harder at me; her eyes fill with tears.

"Autumn, what's the matter?" I ask. "What's happened? Has something happened to Mikey since this morning?"

"Since this *morning*?"

"Well—at all, then?"

Autumn rubs the back of her hand across her eyes and wipes her sleeve against her nose. "You really want me to spell out where Mikey is?" she asks.

I nod, biting hard on my lip. I don't trust myself to speak.

"Jenni, Mikey is where he's been for the last year."

For the last year? But he was with them yesterday. I saw him! I don't say anything; I just wait for her to continue.

"He's at the hospital."

I clutch my throat. I think I'm going to be sick. "Why?" I eventually manage to squeeze out.

Autumn shakes her head again. "This is unbelievable, Jenni. *Why?* Where else do you expect him to be?"

"I—I don't know. I don't know why he's in a hospital. What's the matter with him?"

"What's the matter? Jenni, I don't know what you're playing at here, but if you need me to spell it out for you, I will. Mikey's in exactly the same place he's been for a year. In a hospital bed. In a coma."

"Jenni, are you all right?" Autumn's leaning over me, waving a bottle of something strong-smelling over my face. I cough and sit up.

"What happened?" I ask.

"I think you might have fainted," Autumn says. "D'you want to try to get up?"

I sit up and look at her. I try to take everything in and fail miserably.

Autumn helps me up, and I go over to sit on the sofa. She gets a glass of water and sits down next to me. "Drink this," she says. "You'll feel better."

When did she get to be so thoughtful? The Autumn I thought I knew would have slapped me on my arm, told me to pull myself together, and dragged me out on some adventure. She wouldn't be fetching me glasses of water and looking at me with concern.

"Thanks," I say, taking a long drink and letting the cool water slip down my throat. "I feel a bit better now."

She smiles at me—but the smile doesn't reach her dark eyes. They look as though they've got an invisible veil inside them and she's hidden behind it. It's as if what makes her Autumn has slipped out of her.

She points at my neck. "Hey, nice to see you dug

that out." I reach up and touch the friendship necklace that she gave me earlier. "Look, let's forget what happened before, shall we? Start again. Tell me what you've been up to since I last saw you. It's been ages!"

I laugh. "Ages?"

Autumn half smiles, a tiny hint of the old Autumn shining behind her eyes. "Well, at least two days. Ages for you and me."

I rest my forehead heavily on my palm. I need something to steady me. "I saw you —" I look at my watch. Twenty to three. "I saw you a couple of hours ago," I say, virtually choking on my words. They feel like bricks coming out of my mouth. "We were going horseback riding," I add in a dull monotone. "You said don't be late."

Autumn takes a sharp breath. "Not this again." She leans forward and puts a hand out to touch my arm. "Look, Jenni, I don't know what's going on here. You're not playing some kind of trick, are you?"

It's the second time today I've been accused of that. "Do I look like I'm playing a trick, Autumn?" Then it suddenly hits me. Maybe that's what *she's* doing. For the second time today, I latch on to the possibility that this is all one big prank. A terrible, awful, really sick joke. I can hardly believe Autumn would try to pull off something so horrible — but suddenly it's the only solution that makes sense. Autumn loves practical jokes. That *must* be what it is.

"Autumn, are you joking around? Are you pulling my leg?" I ask.

Autumn just looks at me. "Pulling your leg, Jenni?" She gets up and takes my glass into the kitchen. "I'm going to pretend you didn't say that," she says without turning around.

I get up and follow her into the kitchen. I grab her arms. "Autumn," I say. "This is awful. I can't bear it." Then I stop. My head drops into my hands.

She puts the glass down. "What is it?" she asks gently. "What's happened? What's going on, Jen? Is it something at home?"

I shake my head. Better not to try speaking. Any minute now, my words are going to swallow me up, turn me inside out. Maybe I'll disappear, the floor sliding open, and I'll gradually fall away, slip into nothingness. Like my life has done.

I take a deep breath, blowing the air back out through my palms. "Autumn, something really strange has happened."

"What?"

"The last time I saw you . . ."

"The day before yesterday?"

I close my eyes. "This morning."

"I didn't *see* you this morning."

"Yes, you did! Look. Just hear me out, OK?"

"OK," Autumn agrees with a shrug.

I take a breath. "The last time I saw you, it was just before lunch," I say, choosing my words carefully. "We were going horseback riding." Autumn opens her mouth to speak, and I quickly continue before she interrupts me. "You said don't be late. But I *was* late. I couldn't find you. You weren't at the condo. A man told me to come here. And I did. And now I'm here, and nothing makes sense." I look at Autumn. She's staring blankly at me, as though her face is a mask with nothing behind it. My voice is rising, growing tight and sharp as I try to hold myself together. "I don't know what's happening to me." A tear slips out of my eye and runs down my cheek. "I think maybe I'm going crazy."

Autumn takes a step closer and puts her arms around me. "Hey, come on now, it's all right," she says. "It's all OK; we'll work it out."

"How can we work it out?" I wail, tears running freely down my face now. "You don't understand. I've lost my mind. How can anything be all right?"

I can't speak anymore. Autumn holds me tight, and I sob on her shoulder.

Eventually, the sobbing calms down. Autumn's shoulder is wet from my tears. I move away. "Sorry."

"Hey, I'm used to it around here," she says with a wry smile.

"Look, can I use the bathroom?" I ask. "I need to wash my face."

"Of course." Autumn points down the hallway. "Last door on the left."

In the bathroom, I grab some toilet paper and blow my nose. Then I sit down on the side of the bath to gather my thoughts. But I can't. They're too tangled and mangled, and they don't match up with one another, like a drawer full of odd socks.

I get up and turn on the faucet. Nice and cold. Cupping my hands under the water, I glance up at my face.

Horror fills me.

I grab the sink, splashing water all down my front. *It can't be.*

In the mirror, I watch my fingers reach up to touch my face. It's me. But it's not me. Not the me I thought I was. I'm wearing the same clothes. My new blue T-shirt with GORGEOUS written across it. My khaki shorts. My clothes that I suddenly realize feel tighter than usual. With everything else that's been going on, I hadn't even noticed that. And my hair — what's happened to it? It's all gone! Too short to be tied back. I hadn't realized. Why would I? Why didn't Autumn mention it?

I grab at my hair. My fingers run easily through the short curls. I feel the back. The hair's smooth and thin, tickling the back of my neck in wisps.

"You OK in there, Jen?" Autumn calls through the door.

I try to reply. Nothing comes out. I can't tear my eyes away from my face.

"Jen? Are you all right?"

I make a kind of choking noise. It's all I can manage.

"Jenni, I'm coming in, OK?"

As she opens the door, I tear my eyes away from the mirror to look at her. But I'm pointing at it. At the mirror — the lying, tricking mirror. At the face streaked with tears.

The face that is undeniably a year older than it was this morning.

6

"What's wrong, Jenni? What happened?"

"What happened?" I gasp. "Look!" I stab my finger at the mirror.

Autumn looks at the mirror. "What's wrong with it?"

"Not the *mirror!*" I scream. "Me! Look at *me!*"

Autumn takes my hand and talks in that calm manner that she suddenly seems to have developed today and that I've never in my life heard her use before. "Come back into the living room, Jenni. I'll make you a cup of camomile tea."

"I don't want camomile tea!" I yell as the panic surges through my body. "I want to know what's happened to me!"

"Let's just sit down, and we can work out what's going on. It can't be easy for you. It's my fault. I've relied on you too much. It's all gotten to you. Come on. I'll—"

"Is there another mirror?"

"Another—well, yeah. There's one in my bedroom, second door on the right."

"Let me see," I say. I get halfway down the hallway.

But what's the point? I don't need another mirror. My hands can't be lying to me, running through the short crop of hair on my head. My eyes aren't imagining all of this. It's not just me; it's Autumn and her mom and the condo. It's everything.

Autumn's following me to her room. "Go on. Look in my room if you want."

"It doesn't matter," I say flatly.

We go back into the living room, and I flop back onto the sofa.

"Are you all right?" Autumn asks, reaching out a hand to me.

I don't reply. I can't.

"You'll be OK," she goes on. "I'm not going to rely on you so much anymore. The stress has gotten to you."

"What stress?" I mumble.

"All the stress of the last year. You've done so much by helping me look after Mom and Dad and coming to see Mikey with me — none of it's been easy."

I wince at the mention of Mikey's name. Little Mikey in a coma? It's not possible. I saw him yesterday! And now he's gone. Invisible, like his dad.

Wait.

Invisible. Autumn's joke this morning.

"Autumn." I grab the arm of the chair. "Do you remember making that joke about becoming invisible?"

"What joke?"

"Just before. Just — I don't know. When we couldn't find each other. You said maybe you'd become invisible. And we were talking about parallel lives and stuff. Don't you remember?"

Autumn frowns. "Vaguely. I think. But that was ages ago! That was last year, Jenni!"

"It wasn't! It was this morning!"

Autumn takes another of those long breaths. "Jenni, let me look at your head," she says. "I think you might have concussion."

I let her examine me. "Does it hurt?" she asks gently.

"I didn't bang my head," I say calmly. "I don't have a concussion. Why won't you believe me?"

"How can I?" Autumn says. "You're not making any sense!"

I shake my head. She's right. "No, I'm not. Sorry. Maybe I knocked myself out or something. Maybe I'm dreaming."

"Look," she says, getting up. "Why don't we go for a walk?"

"But what about your mom?"

"She'll be OK for a bit. Come on. We need some fresh air."

She's right. I need to get out of this condo.

Autumn pokes her head into her mom's room, then closes the door behind her and softly pads back up the hallway. "She's gone back to bed," she says. "We'll be fine for half an hour or so."

"Right. Let's get out of here."

We walk along the path, down to our place by the river. For a second, it almost feels like normal. Just Autumn and me walking along together, hanging out. And it would be fine if I could somehow walk without seeing anything around me. But everywhere, I see signs of change. Nothing major—nothing that makes much sense when you say it out loud—but just enough to completely disorient me and remind me that my world has spun off to somewhere that I don't recognize. Little things, like the parking lot. There's a fence around it, and each space is labeled with a number. It wasn't like that an hour ago.

And I'm *sure* the trees at the end of Autumn's row are taller. They were little sprigs this morning. And there's a brand-new building behind Autumn's. I'm sure it never used to be there. And the ivy on the reception building — it looks bushier.

Am I imagining it? Has everything changed? It *couldn't* have. But if not, then how can I walk around here every year and not even properly see what's around me?

"When did they do that?" I ask, pointing at the fence in the parking lot.

Autumn shrugs. "Sometime this year, I guess. It was like that when we got here."

"Where's your car? Don't tell me your dad's gone out in it — not if he's drinking."

Autumn scans the parking lot and points to an old Fiesta in the corner. "It's there!" she says.

I swallow hard. It's the final straw. Autumn's dad drove here in a battered old Fiesta?

"That's not your car," I say, but without any conviction. If everything else has changed, why should this be any different?

"Yes, it is," Autumn says.

"But the Porsche —" I say, the words almost catching in my throat. "Your dad loves that car." I try to latch on to one last thread of hope, desperate to find normality somewhere — anywhere! "Did something happen this morning? Is it being serviced or something?"

Autumn lets out a deep breath. "Are you *trying* to upset me, Jenni?" she asks quietly, walking ahead and not turning to look at me. "Because you're doing a really good job."

I run to catch up with her. We've reached the bridge over the river and stand leaning on the railing. "I'm not trying to upset you! I promise. I just —"

Autumn turns and stares at me. "Jenni, he sold it," she says. "You were with me the day they took it. Do you honestly not remember?"

I shake my head, my mouth clamped shut. I don't dare to speak. I hardly dare breathe.

"Jen, I think something serious has happened to you," she says. At last.

"I know. Something really bad has happened. I just don't know what it is."

"I think you've got amnesia. You know, we've talked to lots of doctors this year, and they've told us about all the different coping mechanisms. Maybe this is yours."

I bite away the tears that I can feel welling up and burning the back of my eyes. "Autumn, what happened with the car?" I ask. "Maybe if you tell me, it'll bring a memory back."

Autumn leans back down on the railing, staring at the river as it trickles and bubbles obliviously along below us. She turns back to me. "You promise you don't remember?" she asks again.

"I promise. Tell me what happened."

"It was one of the worst weeks," she begins, then laughs. A dry, cracked laugh with no humor in it. "Although there've been plenty to choose from. On the Monday, Mom got the letter from the gallery saying she'd been fired."

"Why?"

"She'd been taking too many days off to go to the hospital. She spent virtually the whole of the first six months in there. They were pretty understanding at first, but then they said they couldn't afford to keep paying her wages and pay another person to come in and cover her job, too. So they thanked her for all her years of work, gave her another six months' pay, and told her they were letting her go."

"Just like that?"

"Just like that. She built that place from nothing."

"I know." Autumn's parents were very proud of their story. Mrs. Leonard was brought in to run a tiny, struggling art gallery, and she built it into a major exhibition center, selling famous works from around the world — including Autumn's dad's. "What about your dad's work?"

"That was Tuesday's news. His next exhibition got canceled. At least that one wasn't a surprise. He hadn't painted a thing all year, so how could he hand over twenty new works? We all knew it wasn't going to happen."

"I don't know what to say," I murmur, feeling helpless, useless.

"And then on Wednesday, we sold the car and the fancy condo here. Three days; one big demolition job on our lives."

I lean forward on my elbows and cover my face with my hands. *Where was I when all this happened? Why can't I remember?*

"It was only last month that we decided to get this condo. I didn't want to come back. Dad probably doesn't care one way or another *where* we are as long as there's a bar nearby. But Mom — she thought it would be good for us."

"Do you think she was right?" I ask.

Autumn does that dry laugh again. "Look at us, Jen. My best friend has developed amnesia, Mom's shut away in her bedroom, and Dad's done his invisibility act as usual. How good does that sound to you?"

Invisible. That word again. It's how I feel. As though that's what I've been for a year. The world has passed me by, and somehow I wasn't there. I don't like it.

"Autumn, let's move on," I say. I need to keep moving. I need to stop myself from staying still and focusing on what's going on. Keep moving, and don't think too much.

As we get closer to our place, I notice that the families who were here earlier have left. We walk over the last bit of rough path to the bushes. Yesterday you had to pick your way across them, virtually climbing over branches to get to our spot, but now the water is so shallow, there's enough shore to walk around.

I rummage through the pebbles, looking for a flat one. I find one and hand it to Autumn.

She smiles sadly. "I'd forgotten about skipping stones," she says. She goes over to the water's edge and throws it perfectly across the river. It bounces five times.

I pick one up and throw it across the water. It trips over the surface once before flumping into the lake with a plop.

"You're still the stone-skipping champion of the world," I say.

Autumn smiles again. This time it almost seems to reach her eyes, and for a split second things feel normal. Then she turns to me. "Jenni, what are we going to do about this?" she asks.

I bend down and rummage through the stones, looking for some more flat ones. "I don't know. I'm scared."

"Of what?"

"Look, I don't think it's amnesia," I say. "I don't feel any different. It's everything around me that's changed. I feel exactly the same."

"But that's exactly how it is with amnesia!"

"I know," I say, frustration biting at my throat. "But it doesn't *feel* like amnesia. It doesn't feel like I've lost my memory. It's—I don't know. It's too weird."

"What d'you mean?"

"I don't know. Just—it's not as if I've forgotten things. It's as if it's all changed, in a split second. Everything's different from how it was this morning. Except it wasn't this morning. It was a year ago."

Autumn just stares at me.

"I know what you're thinking," I say.

"What am I thinking?"

"That I'm describing amnesia."

Autumn doesn't say anything, but her look says it all.

I sit down on the pebbles. "A whole year," I say quietly, "and I don't remember it."

Autumn sits down beside me. "Look, what's the last thing you *do* remember?" she asks.

"You coming over to our condo," I say woodenly. "We were going horseback riding." My eyes fill with tears as I hang on to this simple, useless fact. "You said don't be late."

"And that's it? That's really the last thing you remember?"

I nod.

"Jen, you swear you're not messing with me?"

"Of course I'm not!"

Autumn breathes a low whistle out through her teeth. "Wow."

We stare at the river in silence. The water glides past, smooth swells running into tiny whirlpools around the bigger rocks.

"It must have been when you fainted," she says after a while. "You must have hit your head. We just didn't realize how bad it was."

"But I'd forgotten stuff before that. I didn't know you were in that condo."

"Maybe you fainted before that, too."

"I don't make a habit of falling down all over the place, you know," I say. "Anyway, I'd have remembered if I'd done that."

Autumn just looks at me.

"OK, maybe I wouldn't have remembered. But it all feels so weird. I can remember this morning so clearly."

"But it *wasn't* this morning," Autumn insists.

"See, even you," I say.

"Even me what?"

I pause. I don't want to hurt her feelings. "You've changed," I say carefully.

"How?"

"You don't believe me. You're looking for a rational explanation."

"Well, of course I am. What — you want me to say you've been abducted by aliens or something?"

"The old Autumn would have said exactly that!"

"Well, the old Autumn didn't know anything about reality," she says flatly. "The old Autumn was quite happy living in a childish make-believe world where bad things didn't happen and where you could make up whatever silly story you liked and tell yourself it was true."

"And the new Autumn?"

Autumn stands up and brushes stones and gravel from her legs. "The new Autumn knows that the world isn't like that," she says. "Come on. We should be getting back. I don't want Mom to wake up in an empty condo."

We head back in silence. My thoughts all seem to be buried under mush, and I don't know how to articulate a single one.

We get to Autumn's door. I know I should offer to go in with her, but I can't face going back in there.

"Listen, I'd better go in on my own, OK? Spend some time with Mom," Autumn says, as if she's read

97

my mind. Or maybe she just doesn't want me around. I wouldn't be surprised. The last thing she needs right now is a best friend who's only adding to her problems.

"See you later?" I ask.

Autumn nods. Her face is empty and lifeless. It's like a mask made from gray cardboard. It's like someone else. Not Autumn. This isn't Autumn.

As she places her hand on the door, I'm desperate for her to turn around, flash me one of her terrific grins, and tell me it's all a big mistake. Her biggest, cleverest, most horrible practical joke.

A tiny part of my brain is still clinging to the hope that she'll get to the door, then turn and scream, "Sucker!"

She doesn't. She goes into the condo and closes the door behind her without turning around to wave.

Now what? I'm stuck in this strange world that I don't recognize, and the one person in the world I'd normally want to share it all with — the one who would usually help me make sense of it, figure it all out with me as though it's a big exciting adventure — isn't there anymore, and I'm standing out on a path on my own.

Which is when it occurs to me: if she's right about it being amnesia because of the shock and everything to do with Mikey, perhaps it's only all the things to do with *her* family that I've forgotten. Perhaps everything will be completely normal with *my* family. Maybe I'll remember everything as soon as I get back to my parents and to Craig. And then once I've remembered everything with them, I'll remember everything to do with Autumn, too.

I know it sounds a bit far-fetched, but the idea makes more sense than anything else that's happened. I find myself practically running back to our condo, excited and relieved that I've got a plan for how to get out of this nightmare.

My legs are like jelly as I stand outside our door.

I reach for the doorknob, my hand shaking, and push the door open. I waver, my hand gripping the doorknob so tight that my fingers turn white.

What if I *never* remember the last year and I'm lost in this confusion forever? What if it's not amnesia, and it's something that I'll never be able to understand or explain to anyone?

What am I going to find in here?

I could turn back now. No one's heard me. I could go. Run away. Go to sleep or something. Maybe if I do that, my memory will be back when I wake up. Maybe this is all a dream! That's why none of it makes sense. It's not even happening!

But I know I'm kidding myself. I'm not dreaming. However crazy and frightening it is, whatever's happening here is real. I have to get to the bottom of it — and whether it gives me all the answers or not, I have to face whatever might be waiting for me in our condo.

I step inside and close the door behind me.

The hallway is filled with junk. That's the first thing. Coats on the floor, shoes everywhere. And a stroller. I stare at it with the same level of amazement as I would if it had just dropped out of a flying saucer in the sky.

And then I go into the living room.

The difference there is almost as shocking as anything I've seen so far. If you knew my parents, you'd understand what I mean.

The condo that's always so ordered, so neat and tidy, with nothing ever out of place, is *littered* with clothes, toys, blankets, scrunched-up tissues, dirty plates, half-empty glasses, plastic bottles, congealed food on plates around the dining-room table, unwashed dishes filling up the sink.

This is not my family's condo. It is absolutely one hundred percent the wrong place. I've walked into the wrong condo—simple as that. It's the only explanation.

I'm about to turn around and walk straight out when someone speaks.

"Jenni, thank goodness you're here," Dad's voice says. I wonder if that's how *everyone* greets each other in this strange new world. I also wonder why the furniture spoke to me with Dad's voice.

And then his head pops up from behind the sofa. "Give me a hand, will you?" he says. "Your mom'll be here any minute. She'll kill us if it's like this when she gets back. You know what she's like."

Do I? I'm not sure I know what anyone's like. I don't think I know anything about *anything* anymore.

Dad grabs a bowl of congealed goo from the floor in front of the sofa, picks up a few tiny items of clothing off the floor, and nudges me on his way past. "Jenni, come on. She'll be back any minute."

I want to ask so many things. I want to ask who all these tiny clothes belong to, since the last time I looked, any baby in this family was still firmly inside Mom's stomach and not going anywhere for at least another month. But then if I really do have amnesia, I suppose things have moved on from then.

I want to ask if we've been ransacked and burglarized since I went out — but I don't want to offend, just in case we haven't.

And I want to ask where Craig is — but after what's happened to Mikey, that question turns into a hard knot of iron and gets stuck in my throat.

So I do the only thing I can: I wash the dishes.

"Thanks, love, you're a star," Dad says, bringing more plates and bowls with congealed mess in them to the sink and giving me a kiss on my shoulder. "Let's get this place as tidy as we can. I don't think I could cope with another of your mom's meltdowns today — you know what I mean?"

"Mm," I say. No, I don't know what he means. Mom's meltdowns? Mom and Dad don't do meltdowns. They talk reasonably and calmly, and they work everything out efficiently and sensibly.

I'm still trying to figure out what Dad could have meant by this when a bloodcurdling scream fills the air. I leap about a foot in the air and drop three plates in the sink in the process, splashing soapy water all over my T-shirt.

"What on earth was — ?" I begin.

"Oh, no — will you get her?" Dad says as he wipes the dining-room table. "She'll probably need changing."

I turn to stare at my dad. I have soapy water all down my front, I have a best friend whose life is in tatters because the most awful thing — which I have no recollection of at all — has happened to her brother, and now I am being asked, perfectly casually, to "change" someone I have no idea exists. How on earth am I meant to respond to that?

"Sure, Dad," I say with a smile, and head upstairs in the direction of the howling, which has now increased to a glass-splitting siren wail.

I check the door to the bedroom I share with Craig. The sight of Dirty Boy's jeans and piles of cars and diggers scattered everywhere makes me sigh with relief. At least some things haven't changed.

The sound is coming from Mom and Dad's room.

My heart is pounding ridiculously heavily in my chest as I gently turn the doorknob and go in. There's a crib in the far corner, mangled sheets hanging over the side, and a teddy bear lying facedown on the bedroom floor next to it.

I pick up the teddy bear and put him back in the crib. As I do, the source of the screaming—a tiny, red-faced, wet-cheeked image of Craig when he was a baby—turns its bright-blue eyes on me and breaks into a smile that feels like the sun coming out from behind the heaviest cloud in the sky. The pink onesie with a fairy on it confirms that Mom was wrong about the baby being a boy.

I smile back, instantly in love with this little person whom I presume is my sister. "Hello, you," I say, lifting what is admittedly a very smelly baby out of the warm crib, and clearing my throat to get beyond the emotion croaking into my voice.

I think of all the times that Mom's called me and Craig her little angels. She always wanted three of us, though. She thinks that's the perfect family. She says that's why cars have two seats in the front and three in the back. That's how it should be; that's nature's way. I always found myself wondering whether car designs and nature have really got that much to do with each other, but I knew there'd be no point in saying anything. When Mom gets something into her head, she can find a million signs that prove she's right.

And now she's got her third little angel.

The baby gurgles and drools onto her chin. I lean forward to kiss her head, breathing in her soft scent as I do.

"You're the best thing that's happened to me today," I whisper into the fluffy wisps of blond hair scattered on her little head.

Clutching her tightly, I fish around in the bag next to her crib for a diaper. Then I lay her down on the bed, tickling her and making her giggle as I remove the cause of the smell, clean her up, and put a fresh diaper on her. I used to do this all the time with Craig. I was only about seven then, but it's still the same now. He'd stare at me and giggle all the way through diaper-changing time, then reach out for me to lift him up afterward, just like my brand-new little sister is doing now.

I hold her close and kiss her plump little cheeks, blowing raspberries on her face to make her giggle even more, and we head downstairs together.

Dad's somehow managed to transform the living room while I've been gone. It looks much more like the Green family household again now. Nothing strewn across the floor. No dirty dishes anywhere. Calm restored.

"Hello, my little pumpkin pie," Dad says to the baby whose name I've suddenly realized I don't even know. It's not exactly the kind of thing I can ask, either. *'Scuse me, Dad, what's my little sister's name again? I've momentarily forgotten; you know how it is.* No, I don't think so. I guess I'll have to call her Pumpkin Pie for now as well.

She reaches her little arms out for Dad, and he takes her from me and kisses her neck with big squishy kisses that make her giggle so much she hiccups.

I smile as I watch them, and for the first time since this nightmare started, I'm almost happy to be here.

Then Dad says something that reminds me why I could never, ever be happy in this new reality.

"Were Autumn and her parents doing OK?"

Once again I have no idea how to answer this. *Oh, yeah, you know — her dad's off drinking, her mom's like a zombie, Autumn's like a ghost of her former self, and Mikey's in a coma. They're fine!*

Luckily, I don't get the chance to reply, as the front door is thrown open and there's a bustling noise in the hallway.

"Phew, just in time, huh?" Dad says to me with a wink. "Now, don't upset your mom, OK?"

Upset my mom? Why would I do that?

"We're home!" The front door slams, and Craig bursts through the door. An elongated version of little Craig. He's shot up. He must be a full head taller than when I last saw him — a few hours ago! His face has thinned out, and he's got two big front teeth where he used to have a gap.

"Guess what?" he says, bursting into the room. "Mom was talking to the new man, and he said we can ride in the front of the train and I can help drive it, 'cause he knows the driver and he said he'll talk to him especially for us."

He plonks himself down an inch away from the TV and switches it on.

"Hi, hon," Mom says to me as she follows Craig into the living room and automatically turns the TV down. Her face is tired and more serious than usual. Her hair is tied up in a neat bun — and she looks as thin as a rake compared to this morning. Well, this morning she was eight months pregnant!

It's only when she goes over to Dad and takes Pumpkin Pie off him that she looks anything like her old self again. It's as though looking at the baby flicks on a light behind Mom's eyes.

"Did you have a nice time, darling?" Dad asks gently.

Mom's busy rearranging the baby's clothes. I must have put her pants back on wrong when I changed her diaper. "Lovely," she says with a quick smile. "Have you changed her?"

"I did it," I said.

Mom turns to Dad. "Did you remember to put the sides up when you put her to bed?"

"Yep," Dad says.

"All the way?"

Dad's voice tightens a touch. "Yes, darling, all the way," he says.

Mom nods. "OK, who wants some juice?" she asks, jogging the baby on her hip as she goes into the kitchen. At the sink, she spins around, the baby on her hip, obliviously twirling mom's hair around her tiny fingers. "Tom, what's this?" she asks, pointing at the dishes that are draining next to the sink.

Dad joins her in the kitchen. "Er . . ."

She hands him the baby and starts gathering things up from the dish rack. "Knives, Tom? You left *knives* lying around?"

"I've only just finished," Dad says, still calm, but with an edge of exasperation creeping into his voice. "They were on the counter before. At least they're clean now."

"Oh, my mistake. You left *clean* knives lying around, and they're in the dish rack, rather than on the counter! Well, that's much better, isn't it? You do know that eighty percent of household accidents occur in the kitchen, don't you?"

"Yes, dear," Dad says. More quietly, he adds, "You've only told me about a hundred times."

Mom just shakes her head as she noisily puts all the knives away. Then she surveys the room, as though checking it for any more potentially life-threatening hazards. Clearly satisfied that there aren't any, she goes back to the fridge and gets the juice out.

"Do you want one?" she asks without looking at either of us.

I glance at Dad and realize for the first time that he looks different, too. Not as different as everyone else, but different nevertheless. More tired. And there are a few spots of gray in his dark hair that I'm sure weren't there this morning. But who knows? This morning's already feeling like a lifetime ago.

"What's up with her?" I mouth at him.

Dad makes a "Just leave it" face at me before handing me the baby and going to join Mom in the kitchen. He gets two cups out of the cupboard, gives her a tiny kiss on her cheek, and smiles gently at her, as though she's an old lady he's helping across the road. "I booked a table," he says.

Mom looks vacantly at him. "Table?"

"For tonight. Our anniversary."

"Oh, yes. That. OK. As long as Jenni's sure about Thea."

Thea? I look at the baby. *Is that you?* "Of course I am," I say, more than happy to spend the evening with my little sister.

Mom glances over at us. "I don't know," she says to Dad. "Can we see how she is later?"

"Jenni will be fine with Thea, and so will Craig, won't you, Craig?"

Craig grunts a reply without looking away from the TV.

Dad puts his arms around Mom's waist. "Darling, they'll be fine. Nothing's going to happen to anyone. We can call them every half an hour just to check. But it's our sixteen-year anniversary, and I would like to take my wife out to celebrate. OK?"

Mom looks at him and finally smiles. "OK," she says. Then she gives him a quick peck on the cheek and wriggles out of his arms so she can pour the juice.

Dad comes back into the living room, and we sit down on the sofa together.

"What's *up* with her?" I ask in a whisper.

"What d'you mean?"

"Why's she being like this? Mom's never moody."

Dad runs a hand through his hair. "What planet are you living on, Jenni? Have you actually been around for the last year?"

"Good question," I say under my breath.

"What?"

I shake my head. "Nothing."

"You know how all the stuff with Mikey's affected her," Dad goes on. "She just needs a bit of time to get back to normal."

Hmm. Don't we all? I kiss Thea on her soft little head and hold her out to Dad. "I'm going out, OK?"

"Do you have to? You only just got back in," he says, taking Thea and cuddling her.

I look around at the room, at all of them, and suddenly I can't take it — any of it. "Yes, I have to," I say.

"Can I come?" Craig asks instantly, breaking away from the TV for the first time since he came in.

"No." I need to be on my own. I've got too many questions racing around in my head to start dealing with Craig.

"Be back in an hour at the latest, all right?" Dad

calls. "I'd like to spend a little time all together before we go to dinner."

"No problem," I say, and I make my escape.

My head's spinning as I walk aimlessly along the path. I keep looking for things that have changed. I'm sure there's a tree missing — and wasn't that blue shed green this morning? Everything's so familiar and yet so different. It's too spooky.

I automatically head over to Autumn's building. But I stop outside her new condo. No, I can't do it. I can't go back to see her. That would be even worse than our place was.

I need something that makes sense to me. Something that can help me work out where my life has gone. But there's nothing that can do that, and nowhere I can go. I'm totally alone and lost in a strange world that isn't my life.

Wait!

Who said that? Someone said almost exactly the same thing — I'm sure of it.

With a shiver that snakes the length of my body, from my head to my toes and back up again, I remember who it was. The woman upstairs, in Autumn's old condo. I remember her words exactly because they were so strange.

No one knows — no one ever knew. Only me. Always lost.

That's exactly how I feel!

Does she . . . could she . . . ? Is it possible that she might know something?

One thing's for sure — I'm not going to get answers anywhere else. If there's a chance she could help, I've got to try asking her.

And before I can talk myself out of it, I'm inside the building and taking the elevator up to Autumn's old condo. The normal elevator, that is. The old one is closed and silent beside it.

"I only want a minute of your time," I say quickly before the woman's had a chance to tell me to go away.

She's holding on to the door, almost hidden behind it, her face peering around the side.

"I've got to understand something," I say. "I need your help."

"Why?" she asks suspiciously. "How on earth could I help you? You've come to make fun of me again, haven't you?"

"No! I haven't. I promise." I can see she's about to close the door in my face — and part of me thinks I might as well give up. But then another part — a new part, a part of me I don't even recognize — speaks up firmly. "Don't shut the door on me. Please. I need someone I can talk to."

She looks at me for a long time, searching my face, her eyes screwed up tight, as though scanning me with a lie detector.

"Very well," she says eventually. Opening her door, she adds, "You can have five minutes."

I follow her into the condo. "I'd offer you a drink, but I've only got rose-hip tea, and you won't want that."

"I'm fine, thanks." I wave away her offer, if that's what it was.

She sits down at the table and points to a chair opposite her. "Now, what can I do for you?" she asks, smoothing down her dress.

"I don't really know," I say.

"Well, that's a fine start, isn't it?"

"I just — it's just that I came here, and then everything changed."

"Everything changed? Now she's not even making sense," the woman says to the room, as though there was an audience sitting on the sofa.

"I came up here. Where Autumn's family comes every year."

"Autumn again. I've told——"

"Where they used to stay," I continue quickly. "Autumn's my friend. Or she was. Well, she still is, but——anyway, I was coming up here to see her."

"Now, listen——what's your name? And please don't say something ridiculous like Spring or Sunshine." She purses her lips together in a tight frown. I wish she didn't seem so annoyed, but then I imagine having some girl turn up at your door for the third time talking absolute nonsense isn't strictly the best way to bring patience and kindness out in people.

"Jenni," I say. "With an *i*."

She raises an eyebrow. "Right. Well, Jenni with an *i,* I'm Mrs. Smith. With an *i,* too, as it happens. Not very original, I know. Not my fault, I'm afraid." Then she smiles a bit.

"It's OK," I say, feeling more stupid every time I open my mouth.

"So tell me, Jenni," Mrs. Smith continues over me. "Why were you so convinced you'd find your friend here?"

"This has always been her family's condo. I just saw her this morning, and she said it was definitely this unit again. I made her tell me the number just to be sure."

Mrs. Smith stares at me for a long time. I stare back. As I do, it's as if I can see past the front she's putting on, right behind it to the woman I met the first time I came here. The kindly, helpful, nice lady — the one who hadn't had some girl show up three times with stories that don't make sense.

"I'm sorry," I say, wanting to make it better for her. Why should she get dragged into my crazy mess? "Look, I got it wrong. I know I did. I just don't understand how or why I'm the only person confused by things that everyone else takes for granted."

Mrs. Smith doesn't say anything. She just keeps staring at me. I feel as if she can see right inside me, all the way into my soul. Can you see the truth in there? *Can you tell me what's happened?*

"Yes, dear," she says, her voice soft like it was the first time. "You just got it wrong. Everyone makes mistakes."

"But I didn't make a —" I begin, and then I stop. What's the point? I don't want to annoy her again.

"They must have changed condos," she goes on. "Your friend is obviously as confused as you are! This is only my first year here." She pauses, her eyelids lowering slightly. "Well, my first for a very long . . ." Suddenly, her eyes go all watery, and she smoothes her dress again and gets up from her seat. "You'll at least have a glass of water, won't you," she says, wiping an arm across her eyes as she goes to run the faucet, "on a hot day like this?"

"I — yes, OK," I say as she brings two glasses to the table. She sits down and stares into her glass.

"So it's your first year here?" I prompt her.

Mrs. Smith glances up at me as if she's just remembered I'm there. "It is, yes," she says briskly. "That's all there is to it, you see? You got it wrong. Your friend changed her condo, told you the wrong number. It happens all the time. I'm sure you'll find her. Why don't you ask someone which unit she has now?"

"I don't need to — I found her!"

Mrs. Smith does this really weird thing. Somehow she manages to look relieved and disappointed all at the same time. "Well, that's wonderful!" she says. "So you *did* make a mistake!"

She says this as though it's a statement, but the way she's looking into my eyes makes it feel like a question, a challenge — a test. *What's the right answer?*

Something inside my stomach is playing leapfrog. Can I really tell her what's going on? I don't even know this woman. What makes me think she can help? Just because she said she's always felt alone? She could have meant *anything* by that. Why on earth did I think she meant that everything around her suddenly skipped forward a year and left her behind? *How* crazy would it sound if I said that out loud!

"Things have changed," I say carefully, watching her face for a reaction.

"It happens, you know. Life moves on. Things do change," Mrs. Smith says back, just as carefully. She tightens her lips. "People get forgotten," she adds, that sharp edge coming back into her voice.

"No, I don't mean that. I mean she's changed a *lot*. And so have I. I'm not who I was. Or I am, but—"

"You're talking in riddles, child," Mrs. Smith says. "Spit it out — what are you trying to tell me?"

"She was a year older than I remember!" I burst out before I can stop myself. "And I am as well! Everything—" I stop to take a breath. "It's all moved on. It's all changed. I've lost a year of my life, and I don't know where it's gone!"

Mrs. Smith looks as though I've slapped her. Her cheeks have gone white, sucked in, her eyes dark and hollow. "You what?" she says in a shaky voice.

"I — I don't know what's happened to the whole

119

of last year," I repeat, less certainly. And then I realize what the look is on her face. She's looking at me as though I'm insane. She thinks I'm a complete and utter crazy loon who shouldn't be allowed to wander around freely.

She stands up and takes a step away from the table. That's it — she's going to call someone and have them take me away. She probably thinks I'm dangerous.

I'm a fool! Just because some lonely woman confessed to me that she's always felt a bit lost, I decide to spill my guts at her kitchen table and make her think I'm a raving lunatic! I have to salvage the situation quickly, before she calls the police and gets someone to cart me away to a psych ward with padlocks on the doors.

I try to smile. "Hey — I'm only joking," I say. "Ha-ha. Just being silly. I mean, obviously I haven't lost a year of my life! Ha-ha, just my little joke."

Mrs. Smith grips the back of her chair. "You were joking?" she whispers, her words tight like a taut piece of old rope that could snap at any moment. *"Joking?"*

I try to smile again. I know I probably look even more like a demented idiot, but just hearing myself say those words — it was crazy to say them out loud. And to a complete stranger as well! What was I *thinking?*

I need to get out of here. I get up and carefully push my chair under the table.

"Look, I'm really sorry," I say. "It was just a joke. A — a dare. Playing around. I'm sorry. It wasn't true. Sorry."

She nods. Her grip has tightened on the back of her chair. She's furious with me for playing a joke on her, and I'm not surprised.

"I'll go, then," I say, backing away to the door. "I'm really sorry," I repeat.

"A dare," she says, her voice trembling.

"Yep. Sorry. Just kids, you know . . . ?"

"Of course."

"I'm sorry," I say one last time. And then, before she has the chance to say another word — or reach for the phone — I grab the doorknob, swing the door open, and get the heck away from there.

My brain is in a scramble as I get to the elevators. I press the button. I can hear electrical whirring sounds behind the door, but the elevator doesn't appear. I feel really bad about making Mrs. Smith think I was playing a joke on her — but what else could I do? It's better than having her think I'm crazy and telling my parents to lock me up.

I'm about to head toward the stairs when I hear a clunking noise behind me. The same clunking noise as earlier. It's the old elevator.

I yank the door open, pull the gate, and step into the elevator. I need to get away from here before Mrs. Smith comes after me or tells anyone what just happened. In fact, I need to get away from everyone.

Clanking and heaving, the elevator slowly takes me back downstairs.

Once outside, I find myself walking up a lane at the back of Riverside Village. I don't even know where I'm going. I'm just walking along in a blind daze, trying to work out what's happened to my life — where it's gone, if I'll ever get it back.

How can I have lost a whole year?

My thoughts jangle as I walk and walk. After a while I realize I've come to an unfamiliar patch at the start of the woods. I'd better get back. Dad said not to stay out long. I need to get back and look after Craig — and Thea. The thought of my little baby sister almost makes me smile.

I quicken my pace and head back to the condo.

"Where on earth have you *been*?" Dad yells before I'm even halfway through the door. He slams it behind me after practically pulling me into the condo. What is his *problem*?

"Sheesh, Dad, I'm not late, am I?"

"Not late? Not *late*?" Dad sputters. "Lydia, get your coat!" he calls to Mom.

"You've got hours still," I say. "What time's the table booked for, anyway?"

"Table? What table?"

"Your anniversary dinner."

Dad stares at me. "You think we're going out for a meal? Craig, come on!"

"I thought it was just the two of you?"

"The two of us? What are you talking about?"

Mom appears in the hall. She leans back against the doorway. "Jenni, where've you been?" she asks gently. Her face is starched white and streaked with damp marks. But that's not the weirdest thing.

The weirdest thing is her stomach. Her huge, round, eight-months-pregnant stomach. "Thea," I say simply, staring at her belly.

Mom pulls a strand of hair out of her eyes. "What?"

"The — the baby."

Mom's hands are wrapped around her stomach, and she winces and closes her eyes.

"Are you OK?" I ask.

She nods, breathing tightly. "Just a bit of cramp," she says. "Come on. We need to go."

I look at Mom, then at Dad. "Go where?" I ask. "Mom, Dad, what's going on?"

"Craig! Turn that television off *now*!" Dad yells. Turning to me, he snaps, "We'll tell you in the car."

"For heaven's sake, Tom. This isn't the kids' fault, you know," Mom says gently.

"*What's* not our fault? Where are we going?" I ask.

They both ignore me. "I know it's not the children's fault," he says. "I'm sorry, all of you. I just think we should get there. They're our best friends."

Mom nods, still holding on to her stomach.

"Mom?" I reach out toward her. "What is it?"

"I'm OK," she says, breathing quickly. "Just a bit of — just the stress. I'm tired. I'm fine, honestly."

Craig finally appears from the living room. Little Craig. The six-year-old Craig of this morning — not the taller Craig I saw the last time I was in this room.

I reach up to touch my hair. I clutch at my head. Long. Tied back. But it's *impossible*!

"Are you ready?" Dad says to Craig, totally unaware of the growing panic snarling in my chest.

As he grabs the car keys from the mantelpiece, Dad says, "Where were you anyway, Jenni? All that fuss you made about going horseback riding, and you didn't even show up."

Horseback riding? My head starts to spin.

"Where were you, Jenni?" Mom and Dad are asking me. I can hear their words, over and over again, blurring, slowing down, speeding up, washing over me. *Where were you, Jenni?*

"I don't know!" I scream eventually, slamming my hands over my ears as Craig walks by me and out onto the path. "I don't *know* where I was! OK? I don't know!"

Dad looks at me and shakes his head. "I don't understand what's going on with you," he says quietly.

Yeah, you and me both, Dad.

Mom suddenly lets out a sharp gasp and grips her stomach again. "Tom, can we get going?" she says. "I'm not doing too good here, and this isn't helping."

Craig runs back into the hallway. "Can I have a cookie?" he pipes up before Dad can answer Mom.

Mom smiles as best she can. "Of course you can, darling."

Dad puts an arm around Mom. "You OK, dear?"

Mom nods. "Let's just get there."

"Yes, let's." He follows Craig into the kitchen. "Come on. Just one, OK?"

"Mom. Will you tell me what's happened?" My voice is coming out about ten octaves higher than usual, and my throat feels as if it's tightened into a narrow knot. "Please. Do you two have to go out somewhere before the meal? I'll stay here with Craig if you want. Do you and Dad need to talk? Have you had a fight?" I'm searching my brain for anything I can think of that could explain the crazy panic around here. "You can go for your dinner on your own if you like, just the two of you. I don't mind."

Mom's looking at me as though I just spoke in a foreign language. Maybe I did. Nothing would surprise me today.

Almost nothing.

"There's been an accident," Mom says carefully. "Don't get too anxious. I'm sure it'll all be OK, but . . ." She pauses.

"But what?" The blood is racing through me, pounding in my temples as I clap a hand over my mouth. I know what she's going to say.

"It's Mikey." She reaches for my free hand, wrapping hers around it. "He went riding with Autumn. His horse. It threw him off."

I nod, squeezing my lips tightly shut.

"We don't really know how badly hurt he is, but

he —" Mom breaks off. A strange sound comes out of her throat, as though she's choking. She swallows. "They thought he was all right. He got worse, very quickly — and then they had to wait. The ambulance was late; no one was there. Jenni, poor little Mikey ended up waiting *two hours*." This time the choke turns into a sob.

"Two hours for what?" I hold my breath as the hallway starts to spin away from me.

"To get to the hospital."

I don't respond. My body has turned to stone.

"I should have been there," Mom whispers. "I could have helped. I could have done something. I was late. The candle museum — it took longer than I thought, and with the baby . . ." Her voice trails away.

"He's in the right place now," I say woodenly.

She shakes her head. "I'm trained in first aid. Your dad and I did the course together. That's the whole point of it. To be there. And I wasn't. I wasn't," she croaks.

I force myself to speak. "You didn't know, Mom. It's not your fault," I say, numb and frozen.

She nods, then pulls a tissue from her pocket. "We need to go now. Are you ready? Are you OK?"

Am I OK? I nearly laugh. The only thing that stops

me is that if I do, I think I'll scream and scream and I won't be able to stop. "Yeah," I make myself say eventually. "Are you?"

She smiles and dabs at her eyes. "Come on. Let's get going."

Dad and Craig are back. "Ready?" Dad asks, then he opens the front door and takes Mom's arm.

Two minutes later, we're on the road. Craig gets a couple of Matchbox cars out of his little backpack. Running them up and down his legs, he crashes them into each other, shouting out action-film sound effects. Dad grips the wheel with white fists and drives to the hospital at nearly twice the speed limit.

No one asks him to slow down.

8

$\mathcal{D}ad's$ at the reception desk, asking for information about Mikey. I'm waiting in the foyer on some blue plastic seats with Mom, who's pretty much doubled over in her seat.

"Mom, are you OK?" I ask.

"I'm fine, hon," she says. "I just want to know that Mikey's all right."

I don't think she looks fine at all, but she obviously doesn't want to talk about it.

Craig's racing his cars up and down along the floor. No one stops him.

Dad's back from the reception desk with a piece of paper in his hand. "Ward eleven," he says. "Follow the orange signs."

We make our way to Ward 11—but when we get there, they tell us that Mikey's been transferred to the

Critical Care Unit. Mom makes that choking noise again when we hear this. "Tom, I need to sit down," she says. She looks really pale.

"Mom, I think you could do with seeing a doctor yourself," I say.

Dad takes her hand. "Lyd, what's wrong?"

"I'm fine. Please stop fussing, everyone. It's only a bit of indigestion; I'm sure I'll live. My best friend's son has just had a terrible accident. Nothing matters right now except that, all right?"

Dad and I exchange glances, and he shrugs. "As long as you're sure."

All I can think about is her words. *Just had an accident.* My head is spinning so hard I'm beginning to feel dizzy. I've seen my baby sister, who Mom probably still thinks is a boy. I've seen Autumn and her parents, their lives in tatters because of what's happening in front of my eyes. But when I saw them, this had happened a year ago!

Even if I've now got my memory back, it would still have happened a year ago. So I know my problem isn't that I've got amnesia. Which just leaves me with one question.

If I didn't lose my memory — what on earth happened to me?

The thoughts fizz and crash in my head, eventually grinding into nothingness. I walk through white corridors, my mind blank like the walls.

"This is it. The Critical Care Unit," Dad reads from a sign over two pale-blue fire doors.

"Are we allowed in?" I ask.

Mom looks around. "I'll check with the nurse." She goes over to the reception desk and talks to a nurse who smiles briskly, tucking her blond hair into a barrette as she nods and points to the fire doors.

Mom comes back toward us. "She says we can see him for a little bit, but he's not awake." She pauses as her voice catches. "His parents have just stepped out to call their families. Autumn's inside."

The nurse is behind her. "I'll come in with you."

"You go," Dad says. "I'll stay out here with Craig."

My legs start to give way as we walk toward the doors. Mikey's going to be on the other side. In a hospital bed. Autumn beside him, not knowing what's going to happen to him.

Mom takes my hand. "You ready to be there for her, Jenni?"

How can I be ready to be there, ready to see what's on the other side of the door, to see the effect it's going to have on Autumn, on her whole family, when one single thought is making my body tremble and almost cave in on itself?

I've already seen it.

Mikey's lying in a bed in the middle of a dark room. He looks tiny, swamped by monitors and machines with dancing lights, jagged lines darting up and down on a computer. Autumn's beside him, leaning over and holding tightly on to his hand. She looks up when we come in, and I rush over and wrap my arms around her.

"Oh, Autumn, I'm so sorry," I say.

Just then an alarm bleeps beside the bed, and I turn to the nurse, panicked. The nurse pats my arm. "It's OK. The beeping is just to give us information. There's nothing wrong."

Nothing wrong? My best friend's brother is lying on his back in a hospital bed, an IV sticking out of his hand, a brace around his neck, bandages on his head. Nothing wrong?

Tears rush into my eyes, spilling out, flowing down my cheeks. I can taste salt as they run into my mouth. Mom's standing next to me, and I grab hold of her hand.

"We can talk to him," Autumn says. "He's asleep

at the moment, so he won't reply. But they've said he can probably hear us. They're taking him away for some tests in a bit."

"Sometimes it can help the patient to hear voices of their friends and family," the nurse says.

I nod as she backs away from the bed, leaving the three of us huddled around Mikey's bed.

I don't know what to say, and I feel so stupid at the thought of speaking to Mikey while he's lying there like this. I try to remember what I normally talk to him about. Computer games? TV shows?

"Hey, apparently there's going to be a new *Star Trek* soon," I say. I look at Autumn and clear my throat, suddenly scared and empty. I've got no words.

"It's OK," Autumn says, trying to smile. She squeezes my hand, and I feel even worse. She shouldn't have to be looking after *me*!

Just then the doors open again, and Mr. and Mrs. Leonard come in.

"Oh, Abby," Mom cries, rushing over to throw her arms around Autumn's mom. She's wearing jeans and a shawl wrapped around her shoulders. It falls loose as they part, but she doesn't adjust it. "I'm so sorry," my mom says.

Mrs. Leonard just looks at her blankly for a minute.

"Not your fault," she says eventually, her voice thick and dark. It sounds so lifeless, like one of those electronic voice machines. She stares down at her son, two solitary tears making wet tracks down her pale face.

The nurse comes up to us. "I'm sorry. We can't have this many people in here at the same time."

"I'll come out with you for a minute," Mrs. Leonard says as Autumn's dad pulls a chair as close to the bed as possible and sits down, lifting Mikey's hand. "My baby boy," he says, his voice choked and raw as the nurse leads the rest of us back outside.

Dad and Craig are sitting across the corridor, reading a comic together. Craig jumps up when he sees us.

"Take him away for a bit, would you?" Mom asks.

Dad picks up Craig's hand. "Come on, big fella. Let's go find the candy machine."

Mrs. Leonard looks blankly over at me as we watch Craig and Dad disappear down the corridor. "Where were you?" she asks in the same electronic voice.

"I — I don't know," I say.

"We waited for you. Waited nearly twenty minutes. Looked for you as well. Thought you'd disappeared into thin air. But you know how Autumn feels about horseback riding. So we went. We had two places booked, and Mikey really wanted to give it a try, so we let him. Just like his sister. He always loved to try something new. . . ." Her voice dies away. "Loves," she corrects herself. "Not loved. It's not as if he's dead!"

The word lingers in the air. *Dead.* No, he isn't. And he won't be, either. However impossible it is, I know what happens — and even though there isn't much I can give them to help at this time, I can at least offer this.

"He won't die," I say quietly.

"That's right," Mom says, clutching her friend's arm. "You've got to be positive, Abby. There's no point fearing the worst."

"No, I know," she replies in a dead voice.

"Has a specialist seen him yet?" Mum asks.

Mrs. Leonard nods. "They're just waiting for the machines to be free, and then he's going for some scans." Her voice breaks as she struggles to continue. "They're doing everything they can to speed it up, but they've got a couple of other emergencies." Her voice cracks on the word. "He wasn't too bad at first, but now he's asleep — oh, I just can't help worrying."

"I should have been there. I should have been there," Mom says, almost to herself.

"Don't blame yourself. You're here now."

"Oh, Abby." Mom pulls her close.

"They've told us not to give up," Mrs. Leonard says, tears rolling onto Mom's shoulder. "They said the next twenty-four hours are critical."

"He's not dead," I say again. "He's not going to die."

Mrs. Leonard pulls away from Mom. "Thank you, love. We need to believe."

I can't bear to see her like this, thinking her son's going to die when I *know* he isn't. I don't know how much comfort it would be if she knew the truth, but at least I know a year from now he's alive. "I don't just believe it," I say. "I *know* it."

I think about the last time I saw Mrs. Leonard in that dark condo. "It's going to be hard," I say. "But he's not going to die."

"Do you really believe that?" she whispers as Mom puts an arm around her shoulder.

"I know it."

"Thank you." She squeezes my arm. "You're right," she says. "We've got to have faith."

I want to tell her it's not just faith; I really do know for sure what's going to happen! But of course I can't tell her that. It's hard enough trying to convince *myself* it's true.

Mom suddenly grabs her stomach again, wincing

as though she's been punched. This time she completely doubles over.

"Lydia?" Mrs. Leonard's forehead creases up as she looks at Mom. "Are you all right?"

Mom nods, gasping with pain. "I'm fine," she says.

"Lydia." Mrs. Leonard looks seriously at Mom.

"It's nothing," Mom replies. "It's hardly important right now. All right?" But then she winces again and seems to be struggling to breathe.

"That's it. I'm getting a doctor," Mrs. Leonard says. She rushes over to the reception desk and talks to the nurses. A moment later, they're by Mom's side. Mom's doing this really weird fast breathing thing and can hardly speak.

"Mrs. Green, we're going to get you to a bed," one of the nurses says.

The other one turns to me. "Can you get your dad, dear?"

I run up the corridor in the direction that Dad and Craig went earlier. Around a bend at the end of the corridor, I spot Dad ambling back toward me with a chocolate-faced Craig.

"Dad! Come quickly — it's Mom!" I say.

Dad grabs Craig's hand and runs toward me.

It all happens really quickly after that. Mom's already

on a gurney by the time we get back to them. Dad hands Craig to me and disappears up the corridor holding her hand as she's wheeled off somewhere.

"Stay here," Dad calls back over his shoulder. "And don't let Craig out of your sight."

Just then there's more beeping from inside Mikey's room. This time it's louder, and it doesn't stop. His dad runs out at the same time as one of the nurses rushes in. A moment later she's back on the reception desk, pressing a button on the wall. "Doctor to CCU. Code blue. Doctor to CCU."

And then they've all gone. Mom and Dad have disappeared around one hospital corner, and the nurse has joined my best friend and her family, sitting on the other side of a hospital door. Two doctors come running around the corner and up the corridor. They don't even see me as they burst into the Critical Care Unit.

I do the only thing I can do.

I stand in the corridor, hold tight on to Craig's hand, and let the tears run freely down my face.

As soon as we get back to the condo, Dad switches on the TV. Mom's still at the hospital. The doctors said she might have gone into early labor, and they wanted to keep an eye on her.

"Can I watch the kids' channel?" Craig asks, settling on the floor with his cars.

"After the news," Dad says.

I make some tea while Dad watches the news and Craig drives his cars all over the furniture. I work in silence. My mind's too full of impossible questions for me to say anything out loud. And Dad certainly won't have any of the answers, so there's no point in trying to say anything.

"Jenni!" Dad leaps off the sofa. "Jenni, come in here!"

He's turning up the TV as I join him in the living room.

"It's the local news," he says. "Look."

There's a close-up shot of a young woman with a horse, holding it by its bridle. They're standing by a river. The horse nudges her with its head while she's talking. It's got a dark-brown nose with a thin white stripe running all the way down. The woman looks serious.

". . . all completely devastated," she's saying. "Angus has never done anything like this before. None of our horses have."

The camera switches to a man in a suit. Young and angular, he holds a microphone close to his mouth as he speaks. "And what happened next?" he asks earnestly.

I edge closer to the television, sitting on the floor, mouth open, right in front of the screen, gawping silently at it. I feel like Craig. Dad's standing silently behind me.

"We were on a trail ride," the woman says. "We were crossing a river near Mile End Farm when it happened. Angus was galloping so fast toward the edge of the field that he didn't even see the river. Just stumbled down the bank, throwing the child off in the process."

"What state was the boy in?"

"Well, that's the thing. We all thought he was fine. He got up, almost right away. He said he'd hurt his head a bit, but other than that, he said he was fine. So he rode back on my horse with me, and another staff member led Angus back alongside her horse. We went nice and slowly back to the stables."

"So when did you realize it was more serious?"

The woman pauses and the camera moves in closer on her face. "When we got back," she says. "I helped him off the horse, and he couldn't stand up. He lost his balance—then he was sick."

"And that was when you called the ambulance?"

The woman nods. "We would have taken him ourselves, but Bob — the other riding instructor — had taken the Jeep, and we'd come back early from the ride, so none of the parents had arrived yet."

Back to the interviewer. "And I believe there was an issue with the ambulance?"

The woman's face flushes. "There was a mix-up with the address. There's a Moor*field* Stables on the other side of town. We're Moor*side*." The woman looks down. "Some of the parents had started to arrive by that point — but we kept thinking the ambulance would be there any minute, so we kept waiting for it. I should have double-checked," she says. "I should have called them as soon as it happened. I should have done *everything* differently."

The camera zooms in even closer on the woman's face. There are tears in her eyes. After a pause, it pans across to the interviewer. "Michael Leonard has been taken to Westchurch Hospital, where his symptoms have worsened. His condition has been described as critical."

My throat closes up.

"Doctors say the next twenty-four hours will determine what this young boy's future is to hold. This is Pete Travers for the evening news."

The room suddenly feels dark. Dad switches off the TV, but we both keep staring at it, as though perhaps it'll come back on and tell us there's been a mistake.

The only noise is Craig whizzing his cars along the radiator and flinging them over the edge to crash onto the floor.

I've been lying in bed for hours, but I can't sleep. I can't stop my mind from whirring and spinning. It's like a carnival ride going around and around too fast to jump off. The thoughts all crowd together: Autumn in the future, lifeless and tired; her mom like a zombie; Mikey in the hospital—all of it awful, and all happening the wrong way.

Everyone older, then younger again. What happened? *How* did it happen?

Stop!

I try a relaxation exercise that Mom once showed me. Focus on my breathing, on the breath coming into my body cold, leaving it warm. Close my eyes, let my tummy swell . . . in . . . out. In . . . out.

It's helping. She has lots of these exercises. She's been using them with the pregnancy. She thinks it helps the baby stay calm.

That's another thing! She's already had the baby.

Or she *had*—or she will. Which is it? I'm jerked awake again, with the thoughts tumbling on top of each other. It's no use. I'm not going to get to sleep.

I switch on my bedside lamp and glance across at Craig. He's sprawled out on his back, arms above his head, breathing in deep grunts, stuffed animals spread out on the pillow, with his favorite, Monkey, lying next to his cheek.

I slide open my bedside drawer and pull out my diary. I write:

I've had the most horrific day of my life. In fact, I've had the two most horrific days of my life—both on the same day!

I write down everything that happened, every single event of the day: going to Autumn's condo and that woman being there, the old elevator, the man telling me to go downstairs, seeing Autumn and her mom in that dark room, rushing to the hospital— everything. I pour it all out, pages and pages of it.

It's only when I stop writing and read it back that I realize something. As a shiver slithers through my body, it comes to me. The moment it all changed.

I know how it happened.

The second a hint of daylight breaks into the room, I'm out of bed. I've spent the whole night lying awake staring at the ceiling, waiting for morning. At least, it feels as though I have. I must have fallen asleep at some point, because I woke up sweating from a bad dream. I was running after Autumn, but she kept running away from me. She ran around a corner and disappeared. When I caught up with her, she'd turned into Mikey. He was laughing as he ran and looking back at me over his shoulder. He didn't know that he was heading toward the edge of a cliff. I kept trying to warn him, but he couldn't hear me. Mom was at the edge of the cliff, holding a baby in the air. Any second, Mikey was going to run into them, and all three would go over the cliff—and then I woke up.

I shake the dream out of my head as I get up. I'd wanted to go out as soon as I'd realized what had happened, but I couldn't. On top of everything, I simply didn't have the nerve to go chasing answers in the middle of a pitch-black night.

Craig's snoring softly. He shuffles and turns over, kicking his quilt to the floor. I lift it and gently place it back over him. Then I get my baggiest jeans and the biggest T-shirt I've got out of the dresser and slip them on. The alarm clock's red lights catch my eye: 6:51.

There's a note on the living-room table.

Hospital called in night. Mom's gone into labor!
Look after Craig. Will be back as soon as poss.
Dad xxx

She's a month early. Is it OK to go into labor so soon? I silently pray that she'll be OK—and then I realize I know she will be. I've seen the baby!

Look after Craig. Does that mean I have to stay here? No. I have to do this. I have to know for sure. And

I won't be long. I scrawl a note for Craig and put it next to Dad's.

Craig, just stepped out to get a few things. Get yourself some breakfast and watch TV and I'll see you soon. Love, Jenni xx

I slink out of the house like a burglar, silently closing the front door behind me, and head for Autumn's building.

The lobby is empty. It looks the same as it's looked every day, the same as it looks every year. The marble walls, the fountain trickling out behind a glass panel, the archway to the first-floor hallway. The elevator. The one we've always used. And next to it, the other one: the one that's never worked. Until yesterday.

I walk toward it and catch my breath. My heart's thumping hard in my chest as I step carefully inside and slide the doors closed behind me, slicing away the light. I can't see the buttons properly. I fumble along the walls, the numbers slowly growing clearer as my eyes get used to the dim light. My body is alive with prickles zinging up and down, lighting up every nerve ending in my back, my neck, my arms.

I know it's impossible. I know it can't be true. But I also know it *is* true. It happened; there's no other explanation.

The elevator didn't only take me up a floor — it took me up a year as well.

What if Autumn had lived on the third floor and I'd gone up two floors to see her? Would it have taken me forward two years instead of one?

Perhaps another year on from that awful time, things will get back to normal. Perhaps we'll all be happy again.

I need to know.

The buttons are clearly visible now that my eyes have gotten used to the gloom. As I stare at them, I know there's only one way to answer the questions shooting around my mind.

With a shaking arm, I reach out, and press the button marked 3.

The elevator stops. I drag the doors open, run to the hallway, and check the condo numbers: 310, 311, 312 . . .

I run down the stairs. At the second floor, I pause and look down toward Autumn's old condo. Before I've even thought about it, I'm marching along the hallway. I'm not going to wimp out this time. I need to ask some straight questions — and I need some honest answers.

I stop outside unit 210. My chest feels as though there's someone inside it, banging their fists on my ribs. I knock three times on the door, and a second later it flies open.

"It's you! I *knew* you'd come back!" Mrs. Smith smiles broadly and grabs me. She pulls me toward her, squashing me in a tight, bony hug.

I pull away. "What's that about?" I ask, stepping back to look at her. Is she older? It's hard to tell. She's wearing different clothes but —

That's when I realize. My clothes. I look down at my exposed ankles, my jeans stopping a good two inches short of my shoes, my wrists bare where my T-shirt sleeves stops.

"Come on in, Jenni." Mrs. Smith holds the door open for me.

"Can I use your bathroom?" I ask. I need to be sure. She motions me into the condo.

In the bathroom, I stare at myself. It's *so* weird. It's as if I'm looking at myself, but looking at someone else at the same time. It's hard to even put my finger on what's different. My face looks about the same. A bit thinner, perhaps. My hair's still quite short, but it's got tinges of color in it. Highlights? Mom's let me dye my hair? Well, that's one good thing, anyway. It suits me.

This is me at fourteen. This is what I'll look like. I can't stop staring.

"You all right in there, Jenni?"

I haven't got time to sit around examining my looks! I need to sort this out. "Coming," I call.

She's waiting for me at the kitchen table, a couple of glasses of orange juice in front of her. She points to one of them. "I got you some juice," she says with a nervous laugh. "Not just water like last time."

I sit down. "Thanks," I say, taking a sip.

She watches me drink. "About last time," she says. "I'm sorry I was so awful to you."

"You weren't awful," I say quickly.

She shakes her head. "No, I was. Jenni. Please let me apologize." She smiles, and her eyes are so full of sadness and regret that I instantly want to give her whatever she needs.

"OK," I say. "Thank you."

"I thought you were playing a joke on me, you see. But then the more I thought about it, the more convinced I became that I was wrong—and then it was too late to do anything about it. I prayed you would come back," she says. "I couldn't come to you. Couldn't say what I wanted to say in front of your family and friends. I wanted to tell you everything."

"Tell me what?"

"After you came here . . ."

"Last year?" I ask. I realize I'm holding my breath while I wait for her to answer.

"Yes," she says. "Last year."

My heart thuds to a stop. I thought she knew the truth. I must have misunderstood her. "But —"

"Or in your case" — Mrs. Smith leans forward and peers into my face — "yesterday."

"Really? You know?" I swallow hard.

"Yes — I know it all," she says in a whisper. "I probably knew the first time you came around. I wasn't going to admit it, though. Not to you at any rate, not even to myself. I mean, it's not possible, is it?"

"No," I say numbly. *She understands! She believes me!*

Mrs. Smith holds my eyes with her gaze. For a long time, neither of us says anything. Then she takes a quick breath and speaks quickly. "You lost a year, didn't you? The rest of the world carried on, leaving you behind — and you don't know where it went or how to get back. And it happened right here." She leans forward, sliding my glass out of the way to take hold of my hands. "It's true, isn't it?" she says, her eyes as tight as her voice. "I'm not just a rambling old fool. Tell me I'm not. Tell me I haven't lost my mind, Jenni. Tell me it really happened."

"I . . . How did you know I was telling the truth? What made you so certain I wasn't playing a trick on you?"

Her grip tightens on my hand. "It is true, then?"

I nod. "Yes, it's true," I say.

She gets up from her chair, crossing to the kitchen sink. Looking out the window, she carries on almost to herself, as though she's forgotten I'm there. "How could I explain it? How do you explain something that makes no sense at all?"

"You—you—how . . . ?" I can't finish the question. I don't even know what I'm trying to ask.

"How did I know it had really happened to you as you said?" She smiles sadly. "I saw it in your eyes. The shock, the disbelief, the questions. I've only ever seen that expression once in my life." She looks up at me. "And you know when that was, don't you?"

I suddenly realize what she's saying. At least I think I do. . . .

"It was when I saw my own reflection," she says.

"How do you explain something like that? I was just a child, like you. I had no idea what was going on, no one to explain. I couldn't tell anyone." She slides back into her chair, facing me. "Do you understand, Jenni? No one. No way of knowing what had happened, how, why . . . nothing. A year of my life gone. And all I knew was this: it happened here."

"You came here as a child? But I didn't think this place existed then."

"It didn't. Not like this, anyway. It was a hotel. Did you know that?"

I shake my head.

"Just this building. The rest has been built around it over the years. Dilapidated little place it was, back then. My parents brought us here every year."

"So what happened?" I ask.

"I was thirteen years old. Nearly fourteen. Always wanting to be older, wishing my life away. If only I'd known. I remember the night before it happened. I'd been reading a book about a girl who traveled back in time, and I thought wouldn't it be marvelous to be able to travel through time?"

That was what I'd done too! When it happened, I'd just been wishing I could see into the future!

"We always celebrated my birthday here at the

hotel," Mrs. Smith continues. "I'd been out with my friends in the afternoon, and I came back home to our room. As soon as I walked in the door, I knew something was wrong. Celebrations were taking place — but they were the wrong ones."

"The wrong ones?"

"The cards. The first one was from my grandparents. I thought they'd made a mistake. *Happy Birthday, darling granddaughter. Fifteen today.* I showed it to my mother, laughing. Said to her, look what they've gone and done. She gave me a strange look. Open the rest of your cards, she said. So I did. I tore the next one open. It was from my auntie Gladys and uncle Frank."

"And it was the same?"

She nods. "Fifteen today. All of them. It wasn't funny after a while. Wasn't funny at all."

"And then you saw yourself?"

"I'll never forget it, as long as I live. Mother had given me a hairbrush set. It was beautiful. Gold trimmings and padded on the back with a picture of an old English sheepdog." She pauses. "There was a hand mirror. That was when I knew for sure. One look. Dropped the mirror right out of my hands. It smashed to pieces right there on the table. Mother was angry."

"Seven years' bad luck," I murmur.

"Oh, I had much more than that, Jenni. That was just the start of it. Anyway, I went to the bathroom, tried to calm myself down."

"Just like me," I say. "And it made it worse?"

"Absolutely. Seeing my reflection like that. It was like a funhouse hall of mirrors. Looking at yourself, but it's not really yourself, not the person you know. It's a freaky distortion, a shadow stretched by late-afternoon sun. Or a hallucination, a nightmare. You try to peer at it sideways, try to catch it out. But it won't be caught."

"So then what happened?"

"When I came back out, my parents had put the cards up on the mantelpiece. They thought it would cheer me up. Well, they had no idea what was going on, did they? All they could see was that I was unhappy. So they tried to make it better. You know what I did?"

I shake my head.

"Tore them all down. Wiped them off the ledge, then I ripped them into shreds. Every last one. Screaming all the while. Nearly smashed the whole place up. I thought I was losing my mind. So did my parents. They were so worried, for a while at any rate."

"Why only for a while?"

Mrs. Smith reaches down to brush invisible crumbs from her dress. "I gave in, eventually. Played along."

"What do you mean 'played along'? What did you do?"

She lets out a heavy sigh. "After a couple of weeks, I told them I'd made the whole thing up, that it was all about trying to get attention. What else could I do? I couldn't keep putting them through that anguish, so I made up a lie that they were happy to believe — *desperate* to believe. And then I kept on lying. Said I remembered everything. Told them everything was normal, apologized, got on with my life."

"With your new life, a year ahead of the one you knew?" •

"Exactly. It got easier, you know. It does. The gaps are easy to fill in. You just have to learn how to do it. Ask the right questions, in the right way, and people will tell you everything you need to know." She turns away, but not before I've noticed that the edges of her eyes are damp. "Or nearly everything."

"What d'you mean?"

"I mean, you can lie to others; you can even lie to yourself. You can very nearly convince yourself things aren't really how you see them, didn't really happen, haven't sent you to the very edge of your sanity. But I'll tell you something, Jenni."

"What?" I hold my breath.

"You can't lie to your spirit." She clenches her teeth, raising her head in a defiant nod. "When you try to do that, you die inside, Jenni."

"Is that what you did?"

She tightens her jaw. "I didn't just lose a year. I lost everything." She half smiles as she looks out the window. "I was in love with him. I was going to tell him that night."

"In love with who?"

"I said to myself, once I'm fourteen, I'll tell him. Every year, I saw him. I knew he was the one. Right from the start. But I thought, you can't be in love at ten years old, or eleven or twelve or even thirteen. That's what they all said, anyway. My parents laughed at me. My friends thought I was crazy. Boys! They weren't interested in *boys*! Well, neither was I, really. Not boys. Just the one boy. I told myself, as soon as I'm fourteen, I'm going to tell him."

"Why fourteen?"

She shakes her head. "I've asked myself that a thousand times. I don't know. It just sounded older. Old enough. And I thought, if he feels the same way, we'll get married someday, and then we'll be together forever. Every day, every week, not just one week out of fifty-two."

"So what happened?"

"I'd seen him the night before. He tried to kiss me. Well, he'd kissed me before, on my cheek. Lots of times. But it was different this time, I knew it was. He leaned right forward toward me, closed his eyes . . ."

"And?"

"And I ducked. Jerked away from him. You should have seen his face. Looked as though I'd slapped him. I said, 'No, don't kiss me yet. Not till tomorrow.' 'What happens tomorrow?' he asked. I said, 'It's my birthday. I'll be grown up tomorrow. You can kiss me then.'"

"What did he say?"

"He said I was making excuses. Said I didn't really want him to kiss me, and if that was how I felt, then he wouldn't bother. I told him, 'No, you've got it all wrong!' but he stormed off." She tears her gaze away from the window and turns to me. "I wanted it to be special, you see. I had it all planned. I had to be fourteen. I'd convinced myself of that, for some stupid,

stupid reason. I was going to tell him I was in love with him. It was going to be perfect."

"And?"

"He never tried again."

"To kiss you?"

"Next time I saw him, I'd lost a year. He hardly spoke to me. Kept walking past me, holding hands with another girl. He stopped to kiss *her* once, right in front of me. I saw his eyes, though. Open, they were, right there as he kissed her. *See,* he was saying. *I can get kisses if I want them.*"

"But didn't you tell him?"

Mrs. Smith laughs drily. "Tell him? Tell him what? That I was sorry but I'd accidentally lost a year of my life and could we pick where we left off? Think he'd have taken me seriously? Anyway, I did try actually. Just once."

"What did you say?"

"I told him I hadn't meant to push him away that time. Said I wasn't rejecting him. Told him I couldn't really remember what had happened afterward, and I tried to get him to tell me — to help me fill in the blanks."

"What did he say?"

"He told me I'd said the same thing before, and he wasn't going to suddenly give me a different reply now. I could only assume he meant that in the year I had no recollection of, I'd tried to explain what had happened that night. But it was obvious he wasn't having any of it. He told me to let him get on with his life. I said I didn't want him to get on with anything."

"And what did he say to that?"

"He started getting angry then. Asked if I thought he was going to hang around while I made a fool of him again and told me I didn't need to feel sorry for him. Said he had a new girlfriend now, so I didn't need to worry about him bothering me anymore."

"So he never knew what really happened?"

Mrs. Smith shakes her head. "I remember the conversation where I tried to explain it to him as if it were yesterday. We were standing in the foyer downstairs, in front of the elevator."

"The elevator!" I gasp. *Does she know that was how it happened?*

"As we stood there, I suddenly realized — that was it," she continues before I get the chance to say anything. "The moment things had changed. It was the elevator! I grabbed his hand and dragged him inside with me. Told him what I suspected. Told him all of it. I was so happy! All we had to do was go back a year — together. Everything was going to be OK. More than OK — it was going to be wonderful! I was going to get my life back. And he would get to live that year all over again — but as my boyfriend this time!"

"So what happened?" I ask, entranced.

Mrs. Smith pauses for a long time. "He looked into my eyes so hard and so deep that I mistook his look. I thought it was excitement, passion — a realization that we could have everything we wanted, everything we had talked about."

"And what was it?"

"I don't know. Fury, hurt," she says flatly. "Do you know what he did, Jenni?"

I shake my head, anxious for her to go on.

"He got out the penknife he always carried around with him in his pocket and went over to the control box in the corner of the elevator. Working at the edge of it with his knife, he levered it open. And then, before I even knew what was happening, he switched to the sharpest blade, reached into the box, and pulled out the wires inside it. Then he said, 'This is what I think of your nonsense,' and cut every wire in the box. 'No one makes a fool of me and then comes back to gloat about it,' he said."

"But that's horrible of him!" I butt in.

Mrs. Smith shakes her head. "It sounds it. But it wasn't like him at all. He was always so gentle and kind. He was hurt, Jenni. He needed to hit back at me and didn't know any other way to do it. Don't think badly of him."

"OK. I understand," I say quietly. "So then what happened?"

"I said, 'I'm *not* gloating, Bobby — I *promise* I'm not.' But he never believed me. All he knew was that I'd rejected him and that was that. He'd had a whole year to think about it. A year that I had no recollection of — a year of my life that took place without me!"

"With everyone around you acting as though you've spent the last year with them — but you don't know anything about it. It's awful, isn't it?"

"Worse than awful," Mrs. Smith agrees.

"But I still don't understand how it works," I say. "I mean, if the missing year existed for everyone around us, but not for you or me, then was that year real? Did it happen or not? And what about the past that you've left behind? Do you disappear from that completely or keep on existing in two places at the same time?"

"Jenni, I've spent over thirty years asking myself questions like these. I know that you can't disappear from the past completely, or else by the time I turned up on my fifteenth birthday, they'd have had search parties out looking for me for the last twelve months!"

"But if I didn't disappear, why didn't I turn up at Autumn's house to go horseback riding?"

Mrs. Smith shakes her head. "There could be a hundred different answers to that question. Perhaps you *do* disappear, just for a short while, as you travel from one time to another. Or perhaps we both just slipped into a timeline that was always there and was always going to be there, and no one disappeared from anywhere. Perhaps the past kind of starts again once you land in the future."

"The past with all the parts we'll never know about because we simply weren't there to experience them," I add.

"Exactly. The truth could even be that Jenni from a year ago was called away by someone before she got to Autumn's condo," Mrs. Smith goes on. "Maybe she got distracted for ten minutes, and by the time she got to Autumn's, it was too late and they'd gone without her. The fact of the matter is . . ." She pauses for a moment.

"That I'm never going to know," I finish for her.

"I don't think you ever will," she agrees. "Just as I'll never know exactly what happened in my missing year, either. But I'll tell you something else I've discovered. It doesn't matter! There are *always* going to be some questions you can answer and some that you can't, which will drive you crazy if you keep trying. Not all questions *have* an answer, Jenni — and even with the ones that do, not all of their answers make sense to our simple human minds."

She's right. Understanding the ins and outs of exactly why and how this has happened isn't important. What matters is the fact that it *has*. It happened to Mrs. Smith; it's happened to me.

And however complicated and impossible all of this is, there's one simple truth at the heart of it. Both of us ended up in a future we wished we could change.

My head is swimming. I want to ask her so many things. I want her story to have a happier ending.

"Did you ever see him again?" I ask.

"Never. It was too late. He didn't want me. All I

knew was that as far as he was concerned, I'd rejected him and then tried to make a fool out of him with some ridiculous story. I don't blame him for not believing me. But I wished and wished he would."

"What happened next?"

"I was so upset, my parents cut the vacation short. It put them off the place for good."

"So you never came back?"

"Never. At least, not till last year, when you saw me."

"Last year? You mean yesterday?" I say without thinking.

"Takes a bit of getting used to, doesn't it?" she says quietly.

"So why did you come back at all?"

She doesn't answer.

"Was it to look for him?" I ask.

"You'll think I'm an old fool. As crazy as my poor parents thought I was back then."

"I won't. I promise."

"Do you know something, Jenni? You are the first person I've told any of this to in my entire life. Do you realize that?"

I try to imagine keeping something like that a secret for my whole life. It would be like always wearing a mask over your face, which everyone believed was the real you. You would be the only person who knew it wasn't — and who knew that you could *never* take it off.

"I'm sorry," I say eventually. I don't know what else to say.

"We had this thing," she says, staring out of the window again. "Used to joke about it. 'We'll come here when we're fifty,' he'd say. 'We'll buy this place and run it together.' 'We'll be married then,' I'd reply, and he'd laugh at me. I never forgot, though. All my life. I mean — yes, of course I moved on. He wasn't my only love. But he was the first — and the deepest — and my heart never gave up the corner it had reserved for him all those years ago. So I did."

"You did what?"

"I came back when I was fifty! There, now. Stupid old fool, like I said. As if he'd be here. As if he'd remember." She shakes her head and laughs. "Can you imagine that? Bought a share in a condo and everything. Couldn't get rid of the darned thing till now."

"Get rid of it?"

"What use is a place like this to someone like me? No, I've sold it. At a loss, of course, but it's nothing compared to the losses I've had. I'll be gone after this week. Won't come here again. Nothing here for me now, is there? Not that there ever was. I know that now." She looks away and seems to be looking far into the distance. "Do you know what I did last night?" she asks with a wry smile.

"What did you do?"

"Wrote him a letter. Silly mumbo jumbo my daughter tells me to do when people upset me. She says write it in a letter, then address it to them, but don't send it. She figures it gets rid of the feelings at least."

She points to a writing pad at the other end of the table. "So I wrote a letter. My daughter says then I have to destroy it, so I will later. I'll go down to the weir and throw the silly thing in. Get him out of my head once and for all, and that'll be that. Over and out."

"You never forgot him," I say quietly.

She shakes her head. "Bobby was the one, Jenni. Was for me, at any rate, even if the feeling wasn't mutual. The one that shone through the others. Sounds like something out of a cheesy movie, doesn't it?"

"So, you never fell in love again?"

"Oh, yes. I got married. Divorced too. Because it *wasn't* a movie. It was real life, and the girl doesn't always get her boy in the real world. I moved on, lived my life. But there's always been a sense of— I don't know, unfinished business, I suppose you'd call it. Knowing that everything could have turned out so differently — and wishing more than anything that I could have that year again and turn it into the life I really wanted."

"The one where you married Bobby?"

She smiles. "I used to write it all over my homework books: Irene Barraclough. I thought it sounded quite nice."

"Barraclough?"

"Bobby Barraclough. That was his name."

My insides turn cold. "But there's a Mr. Barraclough who works here. He did, anyway, two days ago — or rather, two years ago."

"Mr. Barraclough." Her face has turned white. "Bobby Barraclough?"

"I don't know. I've never known his first name. I think he's left now. He said it was going to be his last year. Said he was staying for his fiftieth birthday and then that was it. He'd be off." As I say the words, the cold feeling seeps and snaps its way through my body. *His fiftieth birthday* — was that why he was leaving? Did it have anything to do with Mrs. Smith?

Mrs. Smith is staring at me, the color drained from her cheeks. "Oh, my goodness," she says. "Oh, my goodness."

"What? What is it?"

"His fiftieth. *His* fiftieth. I've been such a fool, even more of a fool than I'd thought. I had my whole life to prepare, and I got it wrong."

"Got what wrong?"

"He was a year older than me! I came a year too late!" She gets up and paces the floor. "It was his last year, you say?"

"I think so."

"And what was he going to do after that?"

"I — I can't remember. I think he said he was going traveling."

"With his family? Was he married?"

I try to remember what I know about him. I've only ever seen him on his own. But then you don't take your wife to work with you, do you? "I don't think so. I don't know," I say eventually. "I'm sorry."

She stops pacing. "No. *I'm* sorry." She tries to smile. "Look at me. Just can't let go, can I? It's over. The silly dream of a silly girl. A silly old woman. There's no going back. It's done now. He's gone. He's moved on, and it's time I did the same."

"But maybe he *hasn't* moved on!" I burst out. "Maybe that's why he was leaving. Maybe that's why he stayed till then — for you!"

She looks at me, a glint of hope in her eyes. Then she shakes her head. "No—I'm not going to get my hopes up over nothing. He's gone now, anyway, even if it *was* as you said—which I very much doubt."

"Come back with me and find out!" I burst out. "The elevator—it's working again!"

"The elevator? So I was right—that's how it happened to you, too?"

I nod. And then I remember something else. "It was the day after he was there."

"Who was there?"

"Mr. Barraclough—he was trying to fix the elevator! Maybe that was why! Maybe he was fixing it for you!" I try to remember what he said to me at the time, but I can't. All I can remember is that he didn't make any sense. But maybe he did! Maybe this was exactly what he was talking about.

Mrs. Smith runs a hand through her hair. Then she shakes her head. "No. I can't do it," she says.

"Why not?"

"Jenni, your theory is full of *if*s. Far too many to hope that all of them would go my way. There's no going back. I've lived all these years with that as a permanent refrain in the background of my life. You cannot go back. You have to go forward."

"But what if you — ?"

She stops me with her hand. "No, I can't do it. Maybe last year, I would have. Even a couple of days ago, perhaps I might have said yes. I might have dared face another humiliating rejection. But not now. Now I realize why I came here again."

"Why's that?"

"To let go. To move on. I've made my peace with all of this, and I'm not going to risk shattering that now. I can't, Jenni. Not at my age."

"But maybe he —"

"No, I can't do it. I won't. My whole life has been about moving forward. I can't go back. And, anyway, I don't believe he'll have given me a moment's thought in the last thirty-some years. Now that I'm here, I can see that even more clearly. He's gone. It's too late. He was just getting his last tasks done before he left this place behind for good — and that is exactly what I'm going to do."

"So what happens now?"

"What happens now is that I pack up, I go home, and I get on with my life. It's about time."

"Will you be OK?"

She picks up the juice glasses and takes them to the sink. Running the faucet, she talks to the window.

"I'll be fine," she says. "I've been all right up to now, haven't I? I'll survive."

As she's talking, my eyes fall on the writing pad. What did she say to him? What's it like to be fifty and in love? I didn't know it was possible!

"Can I see it?" I ask nervously. *Did I really ask that? Jenni Green doesn't ask things like that!* But then I realize — perhaps Jenni Green isn't the same person she used to be. And I don't just mean a haircut and tighter clothes. I mean something more than that — something inside.

Mrs. Smith turns around. "See what?"

"The letter," I say, nervously. And then I have a thought. Or half a thought. I don't even know exactly what the thought is, never mind whether or not I could pull it off. I just know that I have to try to do *something*. I can't shake the feeling that Mr. Barraclough still loves her the way she loves him. I can't persuade her to take the risk and try to find out. But perhaps there's a way *I* can find out. And if I knew what the letter said, maybe somehow that could help. "Can I read it?" I add. "To help me understand what you've been through?"

She dries her hands on a towel and comes back to the table. "Do you know what?" she says, smiling genuinely for the first time since we've been talking. "I've got an even better idea."

Then she picks up the pad, tears off the first three sheets, and hands them to me. "Have it," she says.

I look at the pages of flowery writing in my hand. "Why?"

"I promised myself I'd write the letter and then dispose of it. I didn't specify how. This way, I get rid of the letter — and you have a permanent reminder."

"Of what?" I ask.

"Of what happens if you just accept what happens to you and don't try hard enough to change it. It's too late for me — and maybe it always was. But I don't want you to have a life like mine. Try harder than I did — while you still can!"

I carefully fold her letter in half and put it in my pocket. "Thank you."

Mrs. Smith smiles and wipes her hands on her dress. "There we are now," she says. "It's done. So really I should be thanking *you*."

"I should get back," I say as I stand up. Talking to Mrs. Smith has given me *some* answers, but I need more. I still need to know how things are going to work out for Autumn's family — and for mine.

She holds out her hands to me as I get to my feet.

"Good luck, Jenni. I hope your life turns out differently from mine."

"Thank you," I say as she pulls me toward her and hugs me tight.

"Don't just accept the life you're given," she says at the door. "Question everything. Always attempt the impossible. Be brave. Will you do that, for me, Jenni?"

"I will," I say. "I wish I could do more than that for you."

She reaches out and briefly takes my hand. "I'm OK, Jenni. I'll be fine."

I nod. I try to smile, and then I turn and head for the stairs.

10

There you are!"

I'm just coming out the front of Autumn's building as Mom runs over to me. I took the stairs because I want to stay here, two years ahead. I have to know what's going to happen.

"Come on," Mom says.

"Come on what?"

"We're leaving. I've been looking for you."

"Where are we going?"

Mom sighs. "The dairy farm, Jenni. Craig's in the condo with Thea. I said I'd only be two minutes. Let's get going." She smiles. "I can't wait to see Thea's face when she sees all that ice cream!"

We're outside the first-floor condo that was

Autumn's last year. Is she still there? What's changed? I'm desperate to find out. And I'm desperate to read Mrs. Smith's letter, too. It feels as if it's burning a hole in my pocket, but I can't read it with Mom and Craig around.

"Do I have to go?" I ask.

Mom's face falls completely flat. "I thought you liked doing these things. And I thought you liked being with me."

"I do. Of course I do. It's just I really need to see Autumn."

Mom sighs again. "Oh, Jenni. Can't you leave Autumn to her own devices for one morning? I know it's awful of me to say but . . ."

"But what?"

"Well, I know how much she relies on you—but just this once, can't you let them get on with things and spend some time with us? Especially with Autumn being so unpredictable at the moment. You've said it's been hard lately."

"I have?"

"Well, not in so many words. But I can see that's how you feel. You never come home from her house smiling like you used to." Mom's face colors instantly. "I mean—not that I'd expect you to. I'm sorry. I just

175

sometimes wish we could have a bit of the old Jenni back."

You and me both, Mom!

"She's my best friend," I say.

"I know. Just — well, sometimes it seems like you're acting out of some kind of . . ." Her voice trails away.

"Some kind of what?"

"Oh, I don't know. It's not for me to say. I've been bad enough myself. I'm only just starting to get my own act together, you know, now that your dad and I —" She breaks off and walks away, heading back toward our block. "Come on, let's get going," she says.

I catch up to her. "No, tell me," I say.

Mom stops and turns to me. "OK, I'll say it. Guilt. Like you can never do enough for her, always trying to fix things, make her life better. I mean, I understand — of *course* I do — but sometimes I can't help wondering if it's holding you back from moving on with your own life. It's as though you won't let yourself be happy again until Autumn is." Mom reaches for my hand. "And I don't know if that's going to happen for a long time," she adds softly.

I don't know what to say. All I can think is — *so nothing's changed.*

"Come on. Let's go," Mom says, still holding my hand as we head back to the condo. I walk along numbly beside her. I'll have to leave Autumn and my letter till later. It seems Mom needs me as much as Autumn does this time.

"Is Dad coming?" I ask as we approach our condo.

Mom stops in her tracks. "Jenni, that's not funny," she says, staring at me.

I stare back at her. "What?"

"Of course your dad's not coming."

"Why not?" I ask. In the silence before she replies, I realize I'm holding my breath.

"Oh, Jenni. Please don't start this again."

"Start *what* again?"

"We've been through it so many times. This is *my* week with you and Craig."

My stomach turns cold. "Your week? You . . . you've split up?" I say numbly.

Mom stops on the doorstep, looking into my eyes. "I thought you were all right with this," she says, more gently. "We agreed it was for the best. It's better for you and Craig in the long run, don't you think?"

"What's best?"

"It's not good for you to be in such a tense atmosphere."

"Tense atmosphere? There's *never* a tense atmosphere at home — you and Dad get along great!"

"Jenni, that's kind of you to say — especially since I know a lot of it was my fault. But you don't need to pretend. We all know what it's been like."

"What what's been like?" I ask. *What's happened to my family?*

Mom just shakes her head. "Jenni, where have you been for the past two years?"

"I . . ." *Yeah. Good question, Mom.*

"We've both tried our best, but since, well, you know, since Mikey —"

A sword slices into my chest, and I catch my breath.

"It just hasn't been the same," Mom goes on, oblivious. *Since Mikey what? Is he still alive? What's happened to him?* I can't ask outright. Mom will seriously worry about me then. She's still talking.

"We've both changed, and it's good that we've acknowledged that. Things just aren't right between us anymore. We all know it. This is for the best, Jenni." She takes my hand. "And I've been coping better, with Thea and everything, now that we don't have

178

all the drama. You've said so yourself." She tries to smile. "And we're happier," she says. I don't know if she's convincing herself, but looking at her eyes, she's certainly not convincing me. "At least, we will be," she adds, maybe reading my mind. "It'll take time. But you'll get used to it. We all will."

She turns back to the condo. "Come on. Let's get going. It'll be OK," she adds with half a smile.

Craig slides into the car beside me. He looks so different! He's wearing jeans and a lime-green T-shirt. His hair has been chopped into a crew cut. Trendy little eight-year-old. I can't help smiling. He sticks his tongue out at me as he pulls the door closed.

Thea sits in the little baby seat that I remember using for Craig. She shakes her legs and points out of the window, shouting, "Baa, baa!" every time we pass a sheep, and "Eee orr" when we pass a field of horses. Her innocent delight briefly takes my mind off everything else, and for a few moments in the car, I relax and smile, allowing myself to get lost in her world.

But then we get to the dairy farm, and while we walk around, I can't concentrate on anything. I just want to get back and see Autumn. I can't bear not knowing what's going on with her.

Mom, Craig, and Thea sample virtually every ice-cream flavor between them. Craig has at least three helpings of raspberry, and Mom goes back for seconds of the lavender, the honeycomb, and the chocolate orange and Cointreau. Thea covers every bit of her face and clothing in brightly colored goo, much to everyone's delight.

I get a vanilla ice cream, just so Mom doesn't hassle me and worry if I'm OK. But I can't eat it. My insides are too churned up and my throat feels too thick, so I just take the occasional lick and knock bits of it into the trash can when no one's looking.

I can't stop worrying about what's going to happen when we get back. I can't stop thinking about Autumn and wanting to know what's happened to her and her family. Wishing and hoping and praying that, despite what Mom was saying earlier, things have changed for them. That Mikey's gotten better, that Autumn's OK, that her parents' lives are back on track. Maybe Mom was exaggerating before. Maybe she was wrong. I have to find out. Not only has all that happened, but now it turns out my parents have split up, too! This future world is getting worse and worse. The only good thing about it is Thea. There has to be something else good in this reality. There *has* to be.

But my mind keeps hurling horrible thoughts and questions around. What if I *can't* get back? I keep thinking about how Mrs. Smith got stuck in the future. What if that happens to me, too?

What if the elevator doesn't work again, and then we all have to go home? Maybe if you leave Riverside Village, you can *never* get back to the present day! What if that's what happens to me? I'll be just like her. I'll have lost my life — not just a year, *two* years. I'll never really know what happened and never be happy again. I clench my hands into fists; they're clammy and slippery with fear.

"This is nice, isn't it?" Mom smiles at me. "The four of us out like this?"

I nod, gulping hard. "Mm," I say, trying to twist my face into a smile.

I spend the rest of the morning following the others around in a daze, trying to act normal, trying not to count the seconds till we're back and I can find out what's happened to Autumn.

Come on. Please let's just go back, I say in my mind, over and over again. *Please let everything be OK.*

The second Mom pulls into the parking lot, I throw my door open.

"Hold on, Jen. I haven't even turned the engine off."

"How come Jenni never gets yelled at?" Craig moans. I pinch his leg as I jump out of the car.

"I'll be back soon," I say. "I've just got to check something."

I run around to Autumn's building. As I approach her condo — the new one on the first floor — the door opens and Autumn's dad appears.

"Hey, Jenni," he says. He looks as though he's lost a lot of weight, and his hair's gray, but other than that he looks normal. He even smiles at me.

"Hi, Mr. Leonard," I say nervously. *Is he off to the bar?*

He picks up an easel and a box of paints by the side of the door. "Just off to hang out in the woods for some inspiration," he says. "I thought this would be an appropriate place to get started again. Wish me luck." Then he gestures inside. "She's in there with her mom," he says. "See you later."

I go inside and stop in the hallway. "Hello?" My hands are sweating. What am I going to find here this time?

"In here," Mrs. Leonard shouts back from the living room.

She's plonking a pile of clothes down on the sofa and opening up an ironing board. "I just spotted this in a closet and thought I'd do a bit of ironing," she says. "I can't remember the last time I bothered."

Nor can I. I think the Leonards used to have a cleaner who did things like that. Autumn's mom was always far too glamorous to do *ironing*!

She plugs in the iron and switches it on. "She's in her room," she says. "Go on in. I think you're just what she needs today."

"Today?" I ask. "Why today?"

Mrs. Leonard rolls her eyes. "She's having one of those days. Good thing you're here. You deal with them much better than I do."

Then she goes back to the pile of clothes, and I make my way to Autumn's bedroom. *Those days? What days?* What am I going to face on the other side of this door?

I knock on the door. No reply.

"Autumn?" I push the door open. She's inside. She's sitting on her bed, facing away from me.

"How come you didn't answer?" I ask, trying to keep my voice light, despite the quiver I can feel behind it.

She shrugs.

"Autumn?" I cross the room and stand in front of her. She looks so different. Her face is pale and lean; her beautiful red hair is lank and lifeless, even more so than last time. She looks about ten years older than she is — unless I've gone even further forward than I thought.

She looks up at me. "What are you doing in those old clothes?" she asks.

I look down at myself and feel ridiculous. To Autumn, I'm wearing clothes that are two years out-of-date. "I don't know," I say. I try to sound cheerful. "Anyway, I haven't come by to talk about my clothes!"

"What *have* you come by for?" she asks sullenly.

"I've come by to see you!" I say. "I didn't realize I had to have a reason!"

"*Everything* has a reason," Autumn says. Then in a bitter aside, she adds, "Apparently."

"What d'you mean?" I ask, sitting on the bed next to her.

Autumn shrugs again. "It doesn't matter."

"It does matter. Tell me."

Autumn lets out a heavy breath. "Just something I read in one of Mom's self-help books."

The thought of Autumn's mom reading self-help

books is so far from reality that if it wasn't for the fact that I no longer have any idea what reality is, I would burst out laughing on the spot. But one look at Autumn's face, and laughter is a million light-years away from my thoughts. Her eyes are red; her cheeks are hollow — her whole face looks about as empty as her voice sounds.

"All this. Mom keeps saying there must be a reason for it. As though Mikey being in that hospital bed for the last two years is some kind of test for the family — and she's determined to pass it."

"They both seem to be coping better this —" I nearly say "this year" but stop myself. In Autumn's world, I've spent the last year in her life. I should know what's been going on. But how am I meant to find out without trying to tell her what's really going on with me? I don't think she's got it in her to believe me. Why would she? I can still hardly believe it myself. "Better than they have been," I say eventually.

"I know, it's crazy, isn't it? It's been nearly two months, and they're still determined to hold on to it."

"Two months?" Two months since what? *What else has happened?*

"You know — the whole thing with his eyes."

"Thing with his eyes?" I ask before I can stop myself.

Autumn looks at me. "Opening them in the day and closing them at night."

Can people do that when they're in a coma? Does this mean he's getting better?

Autumn goes on before I can even work out how to respond. "Four times he did it—that was all. Even then, the doctors told us it didn't mean anything. Just a reflex, nothing to do with an improvement in his condition. And I don't know how many times they've told us since. But Mom and Dad don't hear that. All they can think of is that he opened his eyes. They're convinced it must mean something. They're determined to believe it's only a matter of time. Any day now we're going to be jumping around playing happy family again."

Autumn's voice is so brittle, it almost seems to crack the words as she speaks them.

"But that's not a bad thing, is it?" I ask as gently as I can. "It's good to have *some* hope, isn't it?"

Autumn snorts, then shakes her head. "You're as bad as them if you think that."

"Why?"

"It's make-believe," she snaps. "Childish, unrealistic nonsense that everyone goes around telling themselves just to make themselves feel better. And it's pointless, idiotic, and stupid."

I'm so thrown by Autumn's outburst that not only do I not know how to respond, I don't know what to do at all. I'm aware that I'm staring at her with my mouth wide open. I feel as though she's just fired a load of bullets right at my face. Where did all this anger come from?

"I'm sick of everyone pretending it's all going to be OK. I'm *sick* of it. Don't you understand?"

How am I supposed to understand? I don't understand what's happening to my own life. How can I begin to understand what's going on in *hers*?

"Autumn, I don't know what's been happening here," I say.

"What, you mean you haven't actually been with me the whole of the last two years and seen my parents gradually convince themselves everything's going to be fine — when it clearly *isn't*?"

"Actually, that's exactly what I'm telling you," I say. "I haven't been here. I don't know about any of this!" I can feel myself getting frustrated. It's not fair for her to be getting so angry with me. I don't know what's going on! I need to tell her the truth. This is me and Autumn. We tell each other *everything*. Anyway, what have I got to lose?

"Look, do you remember me telling you about losing a year?" I say.

"Hm, let me think. You mean do I remember you trying to make an idiot of me this time last year?" she snaps. "Yes, thank you. And in case you're thinking of trying again, don't waste your time; I'm not interested."

"I'm not making an idiot of you; it's all true!"

"Sure it is. Oh, look." Autumn points out the window. "See that pig flying through the air?"

She has to believe me. I can't stand being in this without her anymore.

"I know how it happened," I say, ignoring her sarcasm. "It's the elevator. It took me forward a year in time, to the exact same week a year ahead — same date, same time of the day. It doesn't just take me up a floor. I went up *two* floors, this time, and I've gone forward *two* years!"

Autumn stares at me as though I'm a piece of trash that's gotten in her way. "Are you finished?"

Please, Autumn. It's me, Jenni — your best friend! I wouldn't joke about something like this. "You've got to believe me!"

"I've got to, have I? And who exactly says I've got to, if you don't mind telling me? I don't recall needing your permission for anything I decide to do."

"Autumn, I . . ." My words trail away and dissolve. It's useless. One look at her face is enough to tell me she's not interested in what I've got to say, even though it's the truth. I shake my head. "Forget it."

I start to walk away, but I stop at the door. What did Mrs. Smith say, about how she found out the things that had happened, the things she'd missed? Ask the right questions, in the right way, and people will tell you everything you need to know. She's right. I have to try harder. I'm not going to just sit back and let all of this happen. The old Jenni might have, but too much has changed, and I've changed with it. I need to try again.

"I don't want to fight with you," I say. Autumn's still looking at me with cold eyes, her arms crossed tightly over her chest. "What's happened to you?" I ask. "What's happened to us? This isn't us."

She looks away.

"You're not even going to answer me?"

"I don't want to fight with you, either," she says finally, her voice softening slightly.

"Then let's not," I say, sitting back down next to

her and reaching out to touch her arm. "We're in this together," I say. "You're my best friend."

Autumn leans her head against my shoulder, and we sit in silence for a while. It's only when I realize that my shoulder is damp that I see she's crying.

"Autumn, what is it?" I ask.

"I just — I just — I don't know how to cope with it all," she gasps, her words bumping out in big sobs. "Everyone else is getting their lives together, and it's only now that mine feels like it's falling apart."

"What d'you mean? Why is your life falling apart?"

Autumn shakes her head and wipes her palm across her eyes. "I can't — I can't stop seeing it," she says eventually.

"Seeing what?"

"Mikey," she says in a whisper. "I dream about the accident every night, and all day he's there in my mind, in his bed. Not moving. He's never going to move again, never going to see me, talk to me. I can't bear it, Jen."

I wrap my arms around her. "Don't say that."

Autumn pushes away from me. "Don't say what — the truth?" she says, her voice suddenly harsh again. "Oh, you're just as bad as them. Why don't you go and talk to my mom instead? You can play pretend together. She can tell you about the miraculous recovery Mikey's going to make, and you can tell her all about your time machine."

She gets up and stands at the window, arms folded, facing away from me. "What do you think it's like knowing that you've ruined your whole family's lives?" she says eventually.

"What? But it wasn't your fault!"

"Oh, really?" Autumn picks up a brush and starts pulling it through her hair. "Like I said, why don't you go and swap pretend stories with my mom? I wouldn't blame you for wanting to spend time with anyone else — why would you want to be with me?"

I stand up and join her at the window, standing in front of her so she has to look at me. "Autumn," I say gently.

"What?"

"I don't believe I'd ever want to spend time with anyone as much as I want to be with you."

Another yank of the brush through her lank hair. "Whatever."

"Maybe it's you who doesn't want to be with me. Maybe you're pushing *me* away."

"How do you work that one out?"

"I dunno. Maybe you want to prove to yourself that no one wants to be around you."

"And why would I want to do that?"

"I don't know. Maybe because you blame yourself for what happened to Mikey, and it's made you think you're such a bad person that no one would want to be with you — and no one can reject you if you reject them first?" I bite into my lip while I wait for her to answer. I've put my finger on it! Maybe I can fix this, get our friendship back on track, mend the whole —

"Well, thanks for your insights, Sigmund Freud," Autumn snaps. "But if I wanted to listen to home-made therapy jargon, I'd go to your mom." She turns her back on me again. "Now, if you don't mind, I think I'd rather you left me in peace."

"Autumn!" I follow her and reach out to touch her arm. She snatches it away. "I don't understand why you're being like this. It feels like you hate me."

"You really want me to explain?"

"Yes," I say, my voice quivering.

She finally turns around to face me, looking flatly into my eyes. "Because you let me down, Jenni. Because you didn't show up. Because I couldn't find you anywhere, so I made Mom take me without you.

Because we'd booked two horses, so Mikey came, too. Because your mom didn't turn up, and the ambulance didn't turn up — and the delays meant that it was too late to do anything. Because —" She stops suddenly.

"Because what?" My voice is a hoarse whisper.

Autumn's eyes are shining as she looks deeply into mine. "Because it happened to *my* brother," she says finally, "not yours."

I open my mouth to reply. Nothing comes out.

"You asked," she says flatly. "And that's your answer. That what you wanted to hear?"

I swallow hard. I still don't even know why I didn't show up. Maybe it was because I'd gone forward in time and the old Jenni disappeared. Maybe it was something else altogether. I'll probably never know, but it doesn't matter anyway. The fact is, I wasn't there and they went without me. Was this whole thing my fault?

"No, I didn't think so," she says. "Now do you understand?"

I find my voice. "I think so. You blame me for it happening, and you wish it had happened to my brother instead of yours. I think that's normal, a natural kind of —"

"Oh, for heaven's sake, Jenni, can't you stop being

so flipping *reasonable?*" she bursts out. "It's me, OK! You were right. It's *me* who pushed you away, *me* who wouldn't see *you*. Me who can't forgive *anyone* for what happened — you, Mom, Dad — and yes, all right, myself! OK? I can't forgive myself." Autumn stops as a sob chokes into her voice.

"Forgive yourself?" I reach out to put my hand on her arm. She doesn't snatch it away. "There's nothing to forgive."

"You don't understand," she croaks.

"What?" I ask softly. "What don't I understand?"

"I egged him on. I made him gallop. He was really nervous, but I said he could do it. I teased him, called him a wimp. So he did it — he galloped — and he fell off. And then I thought he was all right. I didn't insist on getting him to hospital right away. I believed him when he said he was fine. It was *my* fault. Everyone else is dealing with it now. You're OK. Mom and Dad are OK. Everyone's getting on with their lives — and I'm stuck here in this nightmare that I can't stop reliving. Don't you get it?"

"Get what?"

"I hate *everyone* for what happened!" she cries. "I hate everyone for moving on. And I know how unfair that is. But this anger — I can't get rid of it; I can't get it out of me. I'm so filled with it, and there's nothing I can do with it that's reasonable. So there's only one person left to hate. Only one person whose life I can ruin without having to feel even more guilty." She turns her tearstained face toward me.

"Yours," I say blankly.

"Correct. A-plus." She rubs her palm fiercely across her eyes. "Want a prize for that?"

I pull my hand away from her arm. "Why are you being so mean?"

"I've just told you, haven't I? I thought you would understand, would be a good listener like your mom. Funny how wrong you can be about people, isn't it? She turned out not to be so great, either."

"What do you mean by that?" I snap. I can't help it. If she wants to push me away, fine. Let her. But I'm not going to lie down like a doormat just so she can stamp on me — and my mom.

"Driving your dad away like that."

I clutch my stomach. For a moment, I actually think she's hit me — but she's not standing near enough, so I know it was only words. "How dare you," I whisper eventually.

I can't say anything else. My throat is too choked up. Autumn pulls at her hair, for a second looking guilty, maybe even ashamed. Maybe she knows she's gone too far.

"My mom hasn't driven anyone away. They're just having a break. It's a trial. They'll get back together," I say woodenly.

"Yeah, right." Autumn shakes her head. "When are you going to stop living in Fantasy Land, Jen? Hey, maybe *that's* where you've been for the last two years—while you've been pretending you haven't been on planet Earth?"

"I can't believe you're being like this," I say. "I want to help you. I'm trying to be nice, and all you can do is—"

"Oh, lucky me. You've come by to be *nice*. Well, guess what? I don't *need* your help! In fact, I don't need you at all!"

"I—" I back away to the door, and then I stop. What's *happening*? Autumn and I have never done this before. I mean, she can be a bit hotheaded at times, and we have argued over silly things, but we always make up two minutes later. Not this time, though. This feels very different. "I can't handle this, Autumn," I say, opening the door. "Not on top of everything else. I'm sorry."

"That's right!" she calls after me. "Just walk away

from me. Can't take it, can you? Can't deal with the facts, with *me*. Well, you're doing me a favor! I don't want you hanging around me anymore. It's finished, Jenni. Our friendship. Over, OK? Can you get that into your thick head? I don't want to hang out with you anymore. Ever!"

"Fine!" I yell back, my patience running out at last. "You want to cut me out of your life? Go ahead. Think I care? Well, I don't!" I know I don't mean it, and I wish I could snatch the words back — but my voice is tied up in knots, somewhere deep inside my chest.

Autumn looks at me, her face still and hard. "Well, that's settled, then," she says calmly. "Have a nice life." She follows me to the door and slams it shut behind me.

As soon as I've left, I burst into tears. I can't help it. I just can't believe how awful things have turned out. I thought it was bad enough the first time I went forward. This is getting worse and worse.

I head for the elevator. I need to get back to the present day. I've got to get out of this nightmare. I know that all that's waiting for me is another nightmare, but at least it's one that doesn't have years of history I don't know about heaped on top of it.

I climb the stairs up to the third floor so I can get

the elevator back down. But I stop at the top of the stairs.

If I go back, I'll *never* know how things turn out. All I'll be able to do is watch these horrible events unfold, day by day. I can't help wondering where all of this is going to end up. Will I ruin my life like Mrs. Smith did? I feel in my pocket for her letter — a reminder of how badly my life could go wrong if I don't do something about it, and a reminder that I've promised myself I want to somehow find a way to help her, too.

What's to become of all of this? All of us? I'm about to take the letter out of my pocket and read it, when I have a better idea. The letter can wait a bit longer.

There were four floors in the building. I've only been to two so far.

I've got one more chance to find out how the future's going to turn out. One more chance to convince myself it'll all be OK in the end.

I have to know.

I gasp out loud when I see the elevator. It's been cordoned off, sealed with layers of yellow tape, crisscrossing all the way from the floor to the ceiling. I came out in such a hurry earlier, I didn't even turn around to look at it. *When did they do that?*

I quickly look over my shoulder. There's no one around. My heart's trying to leap out of my chest. I've *got* to find out. I've got to know it's all going to be all right at some point.

But what if it isn't? a nagging voice in my head asks. *What if my life just gets worse and worse and worse?*

Either way, isn't it better to know? At least I can prepare myself if I know what's coming.

Another quick look around, and then I tear at the tape, pulling and ripping it off just enough so I can get at the door and press the up button.

Nothing happens. Silence. I rest my head against the door. *Please work, please work.* I bang my fist on the door out of frustration. *What am I going to do?*

And then: a clunking noise, from deep inside the building, cranking upward, whirring slowly toward me. I jump backward as the noise comes closer, and then I pull open the door and drag the gate across.

With the briefest of pauses, I nod to myself. *Come on.* I shut both doors and eye the buttons, staring at them as though they're the enemy.

And then I press *4.* The elevator seems to take forever to go up one floor. Scraping and squeaking, it grinds slowly upward, jumping to a stop with a thud that makes my teeth rattle. How much more of this will it let me do? It seems to be falling apart more and more every time I use it.

The moment I step out of the elevator, there's a crashing noise behind me. It sounds like a clap of thunder or a collapsing building. Instinctively, I hurl myself against the opposite wall, crouching into a tight ball.

But when I open my eyes, there's nothing. Silence. No sign of destruction or yellow tape or anything. *What on earth . . . ?*

It can't be! The elevator — it's disappeared!

I scramble back to where it should be. It's completely gone! Now there's just a blank white wall in place of the old steel doors.

I scratch at the wall, pummeling it with my fists. *What am I going to do?* There's no elevator. I'll be trapped here forever!

How could I have been so stupid? So determined to find things out that I didn't need to know. How could I have thought this would make things any better? Why did I throw away my chance simply to go back and get on with things?

I've lost three years of my life now, and I'll *never* get them back.

$\mathcal{I}$ stumble out of the building and glance around. Everything looks different yet again.

Was that shed always there? Did it used to be painted white? Has the hotel always had that extension? Did that lamppost always exist? Suddenly I'm doubting *everything:* everything I can see as well as everything that's happened to me since we got here. I feel as if I've just gotten off a merry-go-round that's been spinning too fast.

I look along the row of first-floor condos. At least they look the same. Before I realize it, I'm standing outside Autumn's condo, trying to gather my nerve. I need to see her. Whether I'm ever going to get back the years I've lost or not, the only thing I know is that I have to make things right with Autumn.

I keep lifting my hand to knock on the door, then thinking of a hundred reasons why it might not be a good idea. Will she even want to see me? Did we make up last year or have we argued again since then?

There's only one way to find out.

I step closer to the condo. I'm about to knock when the door is thrown open — and Autumn is in front of me. Another year older, different again. Her hair looks more like the old Autumn's, a bit more lively, but her face is harder somehow, more set.

For a second, we stare at each other in silence. She's the first to speak. "What are you doing here?" she says, looking at me as though I've just landed from Mars.

I open my mouth to reply.

"Who you talking to, Autumn?" Another voice comes from the hall before I have a chance to answer. A smiling face follows the voice, peeking around the door. "You!" the voice says. It's Christine! A fifteen-year-old version of the girl Autumn always called Barbie One. What's Autumn doing with *her*?

"What are you doing here?" Christine asks, in an echo of Autumn's still-unanswered question. Why are they both so shocked to see me at my best friend's apartment? *Surely* we made up after that awful fight.

Could it really have been so bad that I walked out of here and didn't come back till now? A year without Autumn? It's unthinkable.

"What's going on?" Someone else comes into the hallway, peering over Autumn's shoulder, before I manage to answer. It's Sally. Barbie Two. They're both plastered in bright eye shadow, hair tied into ridiculous shapes on top of their heads, and wearing designer clothes. What is Autumn *doing* with them? Half of me wants to laugh. The other half of me is staring at three cold faces waiting for me to explain myself.

"I'm here to see Autumn," I say firmly. I'm not going to let them see that I'm nervous. I have nothing to lose anymore. I've already lost three years of my life. Nothing they can do can hurt me — and I'm *not* going to lose Autumn. I won't let that happen. If I have to stay in this awful reality for the rest of my life, then the least I can do is get my best friend back to share it with.

Autumn's eyes open wide. "What for?" she asks, staring at me in confusion.

"What for?" I repeat. "I didn't know I had to have a reason."

Autumn opens her mouth to speak, then glances

at Sally before replying. I'm sure I see Sally give her a quick nod. Since when did Autumn need *Sally's* permission to speak?

Sally decides to speak for her, anyway. "Well, I think you do, actually," she says, "after everything you've done."

"Everything I've—Autumn, can I speak to you on your own?"

Autumn glances at Sally again. "You can say what you have to say in front of my friends," she says, as though she's incapable of talking to me without their approval. "And make it quick," she adds. "We're headed out."

Christine folds her arms, standing possessively behind Autumn. "This should be good," she says.

For a second, I can feel the nerves flutter in my stomach, but I mentally bat them away. I'm not going to let anyone get in the way of my friendship with Autumn—certainly not the Barbies!

I clear my throat. "Look, I don't know why you're so mad at me," I begin.

Sally laughs out loud. "She doesn't know why we're mad. She's even stupider than she looks."

Autumn doesn't say anything. She's looking at me, waiting for me to continue. Her eyes are heavy and sad. She doesn't look angry at all. In fact, she looks like someone I hardly know — someone who gives up, someone who lets other people talk for her, who doesn't have the energy to fight her own battles, who doesn't have any energy at all. That's not Autumn. Not the Autumn I know, anyway.

"I don't know what I've done," I say. I think about what happened only minutes ago. It was the worst argument we've ever had. But that was a year ago in Autumn's life! She can't still be angry over that, can she?

This time Christine speaks. "Oh, so she thinks not being there for someone for a year and then turning up on their doorstep is normal behavior, does she?"

So it's true? We haven't spoken for a year? I can hardly believe it — but I need to take control of the situation, for Autumn's sake as much as mine. As if her life wasn't bad enough before, now she seems to have this pair of numskulls permanently fixed to her sides!

And I wish they'd stop referring to me as "she," as though I'm not here. Why do they keep talking for Autumn, anyway?

"I don't care how long it's been," I say. "I'm here now, and that's what matters." I look Autumn in the eyes and make myself speak as calmly as I can. "Autumn, if I have let you down, if I haven't been there for you, if I've been a bad friend—I'm here to say I'm sorry. I want to start again."

Autumn holds my eyes for ages. It seems the rest of us are all holding our breath while we wait for her response.

"We don't need to listen to this," Christine says eventually. Then she turns to Autumn. "Come on. Let's go."

"Autumn, what do *you* think?" I insist. "You haven't even answered me." But she won't meet my eyes.

"Where are you going?" I ask as they push past me.

"Down to this cool place by the river," Christine says casually.

They mean our place! Mine and Autumn's. I barge down the path after them. "Autumn, that's *our* place!" I shout.

"Ahh, she thinks it's their place," Sally says with a smirk. "How childish." She stops and looks back at me. "Almost as childish as those ridiculous clothes she's wearing."

I look down at myself. My top that was perfectly acceptable this morning is stretched across a body that's three years older than I feel. My arms are bare from the elbows downward and my jeans that were huge when I put them on now look like capris. All my newfound confidence disappears as I realize I probably look like an extra from the cast of *Oliver*.

Christine and Sally are marching ahead with Autumn in between them. They're talking over her to each other. It's as though she's an object that they've been given the responsibility of looking after — not a person whom they care about.

I run to catch up with them. I don't care what they say or how I look; they can't shake me off like a piece of unwanted trash.

"Autumn, let's make up," I say, desperately trying to think of a way to end this nightmare. I can't bear the thought of being stuck in this awful world and not having Autumn by my side. "I'm sorry, I'm sorry for everything I said, everything I did. Please."

Autumn throws a quick look at me as Christine links her arm and practically pulls her down the road. For a moment, Autumn's face softens. She looks as though she might accept my apology. She opens her mouth to speak. Just then, Sally grabs Autumn's other arm, and they march on together. Autumn looks as though she's being carted off by a couple of police officers.

"She doesn't need to be dragged along by the pair of you. She can walk on her own, you know!" I shout.

Autumn stops in her tracks and turns around. "Don't tell Christine and Sally what to do," she says, a flash of anger creeping into her sad eyes. "They're just looking out for me. They're my friends, OK?"

I sigh as she looks away from me again and follow behind them like a stray dog following a stranger in the hope of finding a friend.

As we approach the bridge, a couple of older boys are walking toward us. Christine and Sally nudge each other and flick their hair. "Hi, Darren. Hi, Paul," they say in unison.

"Hi, girls," one of the boys says. He's tall and lanky with floppy blond hair and bright green eyes. The other one smiles at them. Both of them completely ignore Autumn and me.

"We're just taking our friend out for a walk."

"Taking her for a walk? She's not a dog, you know!" I say, for the first time seeing the pair of us united against everyone else. A couple of puppies bouncing around just needing love and understanding. I will Autumn to look at me so we can grin at each other, knowing that we've had the same thought, as we always do.

She doesn't look at me. It hurts so much, I almost cry out.

"Her brother's in a coma," Christine says solemnly to the boys. She sounds proud of herself, as though she's showing them a medal on her collar. "We're making sure she's OK."

Autumn's face reddens, but she doesn't say anything.

The taller boy nods approvingly. "Good for you," he says. Then he looks at Autumn for the first time. He gives her a kind of sympathetic look. "Lucky you've got them, huh?"

"Yeah," Autumn says without conviction.

The boys move on. "See you later, girls."

Christine and Sally giggle and talk in squeaky voices all the rest of the way to the bridge. I want to say something to Autumn, but I don't know what or how. Does she *really* not mind being talked about like that? As though she's some kind of charity case that makes others look good just for spending time with her? Where has all her fight gone, all her life?

When we get to our place by the river, Christine and Sally plonk themselves down on the grass, and

Autumn awkwardly sits down with them. I hover, standing on the outside of the little circle. "So, which one do you want?" Christine asks, with a girlie giggle.

"Darren!" Sally says right away.

"Good! I like Paul! We could go out as a foursome."

They break into huge giggles, and I try to catch Autumn's gaze so I can roll my eyes at her and so she can make a face at me and make me laugh. Once more, she doesn't even look my way.

"What about Autumn?" I ask. "Which one's she having?"

The Barbies both look at me as though I'm a fleck of dirt on a brand-new designer outfit and move on to the next subject. "Who do you think's going to win *Pop Star Sensations*?" Sally asks.

"I love that Gary — he's got the cutest butt," Christine replies. Then, as an afterthought, she turns to Autumn. "Don't you think?"

Autumn swallows before replying. "Yeah, really cute," she says with a smile. But it's not the kind of smile I'm used to seeing from Autumn. It's false and forced. Two things Autumn doesn't do.

I don't even hear their reply. I tune out and stare

at the river. All I can think is, *What on earth is she doing with these airheads?*

Sally looks around and yawns. "I have to say, I'm not sure what's so great about it here. It's boring!" she says. "Let's go to the game room and see if any of the boys are in there!"

Boys again! Is that *all* she thinks about?

"We could skip some stones," I say.

Christine looks at me with such a horrified expression on her face that for a moment I wonder if I've actually said, *Hey, I know — let's run around with nothing on and see if we can spot an alien.*

"I'll pass, thanks," she says, waving a hand dismissively at me.

"Me too," Sally adds.

"Autumn?" I ask. She looks at me. *"Please,"* I say, holding my breath as I silently beg her to leave this awful pair behind and join me by the river.

Autumn looks at the Barbies and then at me. Then she drags herself up. "OK," she says heavily. "Might as well." I only just manage to stop myself from grabbing her in a tight hug.

We head over to the water's edge and pick up a few stones. I throw one across the water, and it plops in after one bounce. Autumn throws hers in, and it skips across the surface beautifully, bouncing on the river six times before slicing into the water.

"Haven't lost your touch, I see," I say, attempting a smile.

Autumn picks up another stone and doesn't reply.

"How can you do this?" I ask.

"Do what?"

"Hang out with *them*?"

Autumn shrugs. "They take my mind off things," she says. "It's better than hanging out on my own."

I want to tell her she doesn't ever need to be on her own — she's got me! But after last time, I know better than to come out with statements that probably don't match her reality, even if they're the bedrock of mine.

And I want to tell her about all the snide looks I've noticed Christine and Sally passing. I'm sure they're whispering about us now, in fact. But I don't want to do anything to give Autumn an excuse to go off on me.

"I still don't get how you can you bear to be with them," I say in the end. "They're so superficial; they're like plastic dolls! They don't care about you."

"Maybe superficial is exactly what I want right

now," Autumn says lifelessly. "If you don't talk about anything that matters, no one can say anything that'll hurt you—and you don't have to talk about the things that are eating away at you from the inside."

I decide not to push it.

"And, anyway, who says they don't care about me?" Autumn goes on. "Why would they hang out with me if they didn't care?"

I shrug, thinking back to the incident with the two boys. "Maybe they want to look good or something. Show off to boys about how sensitive and thoughtful they are."

Autumn turns to me. "Are you trying to make me feel better?" she asks. "Because if you are, you're not doing a very good job."

"I'm sorry. I just don't trust them, and I don't like them," I say. "And I thought you felt the same way."

Autumn talks to the ground. "Yeah, well, my choices got a bit more limited."

I don't know how to reply. I don't know how we got to this point. All I know is we had an awful argument—a year ago. Is that the last time we spoke?

"Autumn, how did we get to this?" I ask carefully.

"Get to what?"

"This. Not being friends. You're my best friend, the

best friend anyone could want in the whole world. I'm sorry about what I said before."

"Before?"

"I mean — last year," I correct myself, feeling ridiculous referring to something that's only just happened as last year. "Is that what this is about?"

Autumn breathes out heavily. "What else is it going to be about?" she asks.

"So that's the last time we spoke?" I hold my breath while I wait for her to answer.

"You've lost your memory now?" she says. "Or perhaps you've just lost another year and gone forward in time again!" She stares at me with a challenge in her eyes. For the first time, there's a hint of life on her face. Is she asking me to tell her the truth or warning me not to even try it? I don't dare risk it again — not when we're actually communicating. I look down and don't say anything.

"Anyway, you know we've talked since then," Autumn goes on. "But it's always ended up the same way, so I'm glad we gave up trying. It was too painful."

"I don't want us to fight," I say. "I never wanted that."

"Too late, Jen. Already happened."

"You seem to hate me," I say. "I don't understand why."

"I don't hate you at all," Autumn says. "I just can't be around you. Being with Sally and Christine takes me away from it all. Being with you just reminds me how much it all hurts."

"And that's why you've pushed me away for the last year."

Autumn shrugs.

As we sit in silence, I try to get my head around what's happening. Try to believe it could really be true. Two days ago we'd both just arrived at Riverside Village. We hugged each other as soon as we met up in the parking lot; we gossiped right here by the river; we wanted to spend every minute together. She was smiling. Always smiling. This isn't Autumn. Something has gone horribly, horribly wrong.

"I wish it wasn't like this," I say eventually.

"Yeah. Me too," Autumn replies wistfully. "But it is. I can't change what happened. No one can. And you know the worst thing?"

"What?"

Autumn pauses for ages. Then almost in a whisper, she says, "I haven't got anyone to talk to about . . ." She stops, swallows hard, then shakes her head. "Forget it," she says.

"About what?"

She turns away and swipes her palm across her eyes. "Nothing."

"Look, I know how hard it's all been for you. I understand—"

"You *don't* know, Jen! You *don't* understand!" Autumn bursts out. "That's just it. *No one* understands. You don't get it at *all*."

"What don't I get?"

"How I feel. What it's like to be me, to have lived my life for the last three years. Was it *you* who sat by your little brother's side, holding his hand so long you couldn't feel your fingers anymore, too scared to let go or fall asleep in case he wasn't there when you woke up? Was it *you* who sat there while a surgeon walked into the room and calmly told your parents that your brother had an internal bleed in his head that had spread too far for them to fix because he wasn't brought to the hospital in time? Was it you who had to hear the words that would break your family into pieces—that your little brother had slipped into a coma and would almost certainly never come out of it?"

I stare at Autumn. I want to hug her, but the person in front of me looks so brittle that if I did, I feel as if it might break her in half. Not that she'd even let me, anyway.

"Three years ago." She looks at her watch. "A couple of hours from now, when the surgeon told us about Mikey. Two p.m. on the dot. Exactly a day after the accident, my family's world fell apart. You gained a little sister on the same day as I lost my little brother."

"You didn't lose —"

"As good as," Autumn says before I can finish my sentence.

I bite my tongue.

"And now it's too late to do anything."

"What do you mean it's too late?" I ask.

Autumn shakes her head. "Forget it. Just don't say you know how hard it's been. OK?" She drops the stones she was holding in her hands and goes over to Christine and Sally. "Are we going back?" she says to them. "I've had enough of it around here."

Sally and Christine get up. "Yeah, come on, let's go back to my place," Sally says. "I'll paint your nails and do your hair, and then we can go to the game room and see who's there."

"Fine. Whatever. Let's just go," Autumn says, and

walks off. Christine and Sally trail behind, giggling and gossiping all the way.

I run to catch up with Autumn. "Autumn. Come on — do your hair? Paint your nails? Going to the game room to check out the boys? That's not the Autumn I know!"

"Look, you're right — I don't want to do those things. It's not me. It's not what I want. OK? Happy? But how can I tell them that? Jenni, don't you see? I'm *not* the Autumn you know anymore. That's the whole point. I hardly know *who* I am anymore. I know they treat me like an idiot most of the time, and I couldn't care less about the silly things they talk about — but what options do I have? I just don't have the strength to tell them to get lost."

You've got me, I want to say. *I can be strong enough for us both, if that's what you need.* I keep my mouth shut, though. I don't want to start another argument.

"And you know what else?" Autumn goes on. "You're not the Jen I thought I knew anymore, either."

I look at her for a long time. "No, I'm not," I say eventually. "And do you know what? It's time I proved it. It's time someone stood up for *both* of us."

I turn around and wait for the Barbies to catch up. "Hey, guess what," I say. "Autumn doesn't want to go to your place. She's not interested in checking out boys who only talk to you because they think you're so kind looking after your poor bereaved friend. And she doesn't need you to do anything to her hair or her nails. She's fine as she is. Oh, and she couldn't give two hoots about *Pop Star Sensation*—and she doesn't even *know* who Gary is, let alone care! So you can keep your stupid, superficial world, and you can forget the 'Oh, we're so kind, we look after the girl whose brother's in a coma' goody-goody-two-shoes act, because she's not buying it anymore—and neither am I!"

The three of them stare at me. For a moment, I think I've gone too far. But Christine and Sally have turned so red, I know I've hit the nail on the head.

Christine flicks her head back. "Don't you start—"

"Yes, I will start!" I cut her off. "And I'll finish." I glance at Autumn. She's staring at me, mouth open, eyes wide. Should I stop? There's something in Autumn's eyes that I don't recognize. Then I realize what it is: admiration, gratitude, even relief. That's all I need to spur me on.

I turn back to Christine and Sally. "You aren't real friends," I say. "You don't truly care about Autumn. You only ever wanted to be with her because she was popular and you thought it'd make you look good to be seen with her, and now you just want to seem to be caring so you can get noticed by a couple of stupid boys."

Sally steps forward. "Now, hang on a minute —"

"No, I won't hang on a minute!" I say, fury and loyalty pushing me on. Someone has to say this — and that someone is going to have to be me. This whole stupid, awful reality has taken so much away from me that I haven't got anything to lose anymore, so I'm going to tell it how it is.

"Autumn's not a badge for you to parade around with so you can pick up brownie points. She's a person — a fantastic person. She's the best friend anyone could want, and if you don't realize that, then you're both even more dumb than I thought!"

Before they have a chance to answer, I turn and stomp up to Autumn. She's gaping at me. "I'm sorry," I say. "I don't want to ruin any of your friendships, and if they truly matter to you, then I'll apologize to them, once I've calmed down. But I had to do that. I'm not going to sit and watch this joke any longer. You matter too much to me for that."

Autumn swallows, looking across at Christine and Sally. She doesn't say anything.

"Listen. I don't want us to fight. I *never* want us to stop being friends," I say. "If you feel the same way, come over to my place later."

Autumn still doesn't answer.

"If you don't come, I'll know you don't want us to be friends and I'll leave you alone. I won't bother you again."

Eventually, she nods.

"OK," I say awkwardly. "I'll leave it up to you." Then I turn and walk away, heading back to our condo and suddenly realizing yet again that I haven't got a clue what's waiting for me when I get there. All I know is that I need to get back to my own territory and find something I can recognize — something that will help me find my way through this crazy, awful world that I've landed in.

I need a place where I can think. I need to be on my own. I need to make a plan.

"That you, Jen?" a woman's voice calls as I close the front door behind me.

I step into the living room. There's a strange woman sitting on the sofa with Dad. "Who are you?" I ask.

Dad puts his paper down. "Jenni. Don't be so rude."

The woman puts her hand on his arm. "It's all right, darling. I don't mind."

"Well, I do," he says. "Jenni, apologize to Karen now."

I stare at them both: Dad's face dark and angry; the strange woman—Karen, apparently—smiling at me through big brown eyes. "She doesn't have to apologize," she says. "We're all right, aren't we, Jen?"

"I don't know who you are," I say before I can stop myself.

Karen sucks in her breath as she half closes her eyes. Then she smiles again. "I'll make a cup of tea," she says, leaning forward to get up.

Dad stops her. "No, you won't," he says firmly. "Not until Jenni apologizes." He turns back to me. "We talked this through. We've all had plenty of time to get used to it, and if Craig can accept Karen, then I think you can, too."

My brain tries to do a quick catch-up on three years' worth of missing facts. *Come on, Jenni. Remember you're fifteen now. Everyone else's world has moved on three years. Get with it!*

"I'm sorry, Karen," I say, trying to get my voice to come out sounding natural. "It was a shock. I just need to get used to it."

"Get used to it?" Dad repeats. "You've had six months! We talked about Karen coming with us. You said you didn't mind."

Six months?

Karen gets up. "I'm going to get that cup of tea," she says, lightly touching my arm as she passes me.

"I thought you liked Karen," Dad says in a lower voice. "I thought you got along well."

"I—I . . ." *Say the right things. Act as if you know what's going on.* "I do," I say eventually. I suppose it's not Dad's fault that as far as I'm concerned, he and Mom were still together yesterday. In my world. In my messed-up, impossible world.

"Well, do you think you could act like you do, please?" Dad says sternly. Then his voice softens a little. "We've talked about it so much. I know it's hard for you — it's hard for me, too, sometimes. You know I'll always love your mom, and it would have been great if we could have made it work. But we didn't — and we're both happy with how things are now. We're happy enough. Can't that be enough for you, too?"

I nod. My head is swimming.

"Thank you." Dad picks up his paper again. "We're having lunch soon, all right? Try to be civil."

"I will," I reply. "Where's Craig?"

"Out with his pals. He'll be back soon."

"Where's Thea?" I ask, suddenly remembering I have a baby sister now.

Dad shoots me a filthy look.

"What?" I ask.

"You know very well that Thea's with your mom. Jenni, please stop trying to make this hard for us."

"I'm not trying—" I let out a heavy breath. "Forget it," I say. "I'm going to my room."

I go to the room I share with Craig and slump down on my bed. His side is a complete mess. Dirty khaki pants, inside-out jeans, and crumpled-up T-shirts litter the floor. There are no stuffed animals on his pillow this year. There's a chemistry set on the floor by his bed.

My side is tidy, the bed made, clothes put away. I sit up and look around. Maybe there'll be a clue some-where. Something that can help all of this to make sense, to fit together. Better still—something that could help me work out how to get back. I feel as though I'm doing a jigsaw puzzle; the only problem is that the pieces are from three different puzzles and they're all mixed up together.

I scavenge through the bits and pieces on the dress-ing table. Most of it's Craig's. Miniature cars broken into pieces with their wheels hanging off, a penknife, screwed-up tissues and bits of paper, a magnifying glass. My side just has a few things on it: a bottle of perfume, two necklaces, some mascara. Mascara! I can't imagine wearing makeup. Dad's always had this thing about me being too young, despite the fact that half the girls in my grade already go to school looking like models. I've only ever put makeup on at Autumn's when I've been staying over so Dad doesn't have to realize his little baby's growing up.

No clues. Nothing to help me work out how to play this new game called my life.

I turn back to the bed and glance at the night-stand. Maybe there'll be something in there. I yank the drawer open. There's a book. I pull it out. Of course — my diary! I scan through the pages for the latest entry. It's dated last Saturday.

I hope Autumn's coming to the condo this week. I wish we could go back to how we were. Maybe there we'll be able to try again. Maybe this time it won't end up in a huge fight. I just don't know how to talk to her anymore. It seems there's nothing I can do that doesn't create an argument. Maybe she's right and we should just stop trying — but I can't. I want her back.

It was awful last Saturday at the club. For once, I was out with Natalie and the others, making a reasonably good attempt at having fun. I'd almost forgotten how miserable this last year has been, but Autumn's face when she saw

me there — it was so horrible. She looked at me
as though I was a rodent that had crawled out
of the drains. It was as if I had no right to be
somewhere that she wanted to be. As if we hadn't
shared everything in our lives like twins up until
the last few years. Natalie said it's best to leave
her. It probably is, but — oh, I don't know. I just
miss her so much.

I wish I could have my life back how it used to
be. Nothing's the same. Nothing will ever be the
same again.

I wish I'd never gone in that stupid elevator.

At least I've got the letter. No one knows
about that. I know I'll find Mrs. Smith again one
day — and maybe then we can help each other
out of this mess. Maybe if I can help her to be
happy, this can all be different. If I could just do
one thing right.

The letter! Of course! I've been so wrapped up
with everything to do with Autumn that I'd forgotten
all about it! I still don't even know what it says.

I reach into my pocket, pull out the pages, and
open them up.

Dear Bobby,

I don't know if you will remember me. In fact, I very much doubt it. I am the girl you spent carefree days with and exchanged childish dreams with many eons ago.

We spent a week of each year together — at the Riverside Hotel — and I have to tell you, those weeks were among the happiest of my life.

Whether you remember those days or not, I wanted to tell you — I have never forgotten them.

In fact, in recent years the memories have played with me and the promises have plagued me. Do you remember our promises?

I should tell you first of all: I have lived a happy-enough life. At least, as happy as it could have been, given my rather unusual circumstances. But more of that later. For now, I want to tell you this, and if it seems somewhat dramatic or obtuse, then at least I don't need to worry about what your reaction may be. I can tell you my true feelings — I can tell you anything at all — because I know that you will never read this letter. And so I am going to tell you the truth — the truth that I have never spoken aloud and that no one has ever known. The secret that has been stored in my heart, like a genie hidden in a bottle.

My secret is that I have always loved you and I always will.

There, I've said it. And it's true. But it's also pointless, and so I am writing this letter to get the feelings out of me and let them rest, before they can take away any more of my years or trap me any longer with the hold they have over me. And so, Bobby, I—

The front door slams. "Back!" a boy's voice shouts. Craig. A moment later his feet thump up the stairs, and I quickly fold the letter, place it in my pocket, and shove my diary in the bedside drawer.

Craig appears at the door. A grown boy, mud all over his T-shirt, spiky, gelled hair, but a still-childish scowl on his face. "What are you doing?" he asks in a grown-up, serious voice.

I get off the bed and pick up some of his clothes. "Cleaning up."

He shrugs. Then he squints at me. "What are you *wearing?*"

I pull at my T-shirt. "I —"

"Lunchtime!" Dad calls from the living room. "Craig, get changed."

Craig pulls a clean shirt out of the closet and disappears into the bathroom. I shut the bedroom door after him, then grab some clothes out of my closet and throw them on, shoving the letter in my pocket. At least I *look* more normal now, even if I don't feel it.

We're just finishing lunch when there's a quiet knock at the door.

"I'll get it." Craig leaps up from the table.

A moment later, he calls me from the hall. "It's Autumn," he says as he sits back down at the table.

"Autumn?" Dad looks surprised. "I thought you two weren't speaking."

"We — we weren't," I mumble as I get up from the table.

"Have you made up again, then?"

"Um. I'm not sure. I think so, maybe," I falter.

"Well, that's nice, isn't it?" Dad says, smiling at Karen.

"OK if I go out?" I ask.

"Of course it is, love." Karen answers this time,

putting a hand on Dad's knee. It feels really weird to see her do that.

"Great." I hurry to the door.

Autumn's waiting outside. She gives me a shy smile as I close the door behind me and follow her out. "Shall we go for a walk?" she asks.

"Definitely!" We walk along in silence for a while, following the path upriver, the opposite way from earlier.

"Look, I'm sorry about before," I say eventually. "I shouldn't have gone off like that. I don't know what came over me."

"Neither do I." Autumn laughs.

I grimace. "I shouldn't have done it," I repeat.

Autumn reaches out to grab my arm. I stop walking. "Yes, you should have," she says seriously. "It was amazing. It was like an electric shock."

"What d'you mean?"

Autumn shakes her head. "I don't know. I feel like you woke me up again. Seeing you like that. You've never done anything like that. It was always me, wasn't it? I'd always take the lead. I'd be the pushy one, telling everyone else what to do."

"Yeah, you could say that," I admit, a smile creeping onto my face.

"I always used to wish I could be more like you."

I nearly fall over in shock. "More like me?" I gasp. "Why on earth would you want to be like *me*?"

Autumn kicks her feet in the gravel as she carries on up the path. "You're so calm and steady. You take things as they come, take people as they are. And they're the same with you. You're easy to please."

"Oh, thanks!"

"No, I don't mean it in a bad way. I mean—I mean, things make you happy really easily, you're laid-back. You don't have to be the center of attention in order to feel good."

"But you're the center of attention because you're so much fun."

Autumn stops again and turns to me. "Do I seem like much fun now?"

I don't reply.

"That's the problem, you see. I've spent my whole life being like that—but I can't do it anymore, and now nothing works."

"What doesn't work?"

"Me. My life," she says. Her voice is dark and empty. "I put on this act, make people think I'm coping, make them think I'm happy enough. I spent the first year after the accident looking after Mom and

232

Dad, the second year falling apart myself, and the third—well, I don't even know where that's gone. It's as if I've disappeared altogether. I've turned into a paper-thin image of who I really am—and you just showed that all up for the pretense it is."

"How did I do that?"

Autumn smiles shyly. "You reminded me what real friendship is."

I can feel my cheeks burning. For a moment, it all feels worth it. Everything I've gone through over these last few days. It *is* all going to work out after all! Even if I end up trapped three years ahead forever, at least I'll have Autumn by my side. We'll be best friends forever. I'll tell her everything, and we'll help each other cope with it all. She'll help me fill in the gaps, and I'll help her deal with everything that's happened to her. A huge weight feels like it's flying off me and into the distance.

And then Autumn speaks again, and the weight boomerangs around and comes back to hit me flat in the stomach.

"But it's not enough," she says.

"What? What isn't enough?"

"Any of it. It's too late."

"I don't understand. Too late for what?"

233

Autumn shakes her head. "For anything," she says eventually. "For everything." Her voice comes out as a squeak, as though the words are being squeezed and strangled in her throat.

"Autumn, what are you talking about?" I repeat, taking a step closer toward her.

She wipes the back of her hand across her face. "I can't — I can't . . . Please, just let it go, Jen."

One look at her tearstained face is all I need to let me know this is serious. "No, I won't let it go," I say firmly. A tiny part of me registers a split second of shock. I've *never* said no to Autumn before!

Autumn looks into my eyes. She takes a deep breath, and when she speaks, her voice is so soft, it's like a whisper on a breeze. "You remember last year, when I was so mean to you? I told you to stop living in a fantasy world? And I was so mad at Mom and Dad for hanging on to the smallest bits of hope?"

"I remember," I say. It's not hard, seeing as it was only a few hours ago in my world.

"Well, I was wrong."

"What do you mean? You were wrong about what?"

"I thought that we'd all do better to face the truth. But I want the fantasy back," she says.

I stop walking and turn to face her. "Autumn, what are you trying to say?"

She stops as well and looks at me. "They've been seeing a counselor for the last year. They've managed to drag me along a few times, too. He's helped them face the facts. Helped us all to come to terms with the reality. With what the doctors have been telling us all for three years. That all we're doing is prolonging the inevitable."

There's a cold feeling that I can't explain slithering around inside my body. It creeps up my spine, snakes along the back of my neck, and comes to settle in my throat. "I don't understand," I say eventually. "What are you trying to tell me?"

Autumn's shoulders shake as she drops her head. Her reply is barely audible. "They wanted us to come here to make the decision — the place where it happened, the last place we were happy together. We talked last night, and we've all agreed. We tried to find a way around it, but we've spent so long clutching at straws, there's nothing left to hold on to."

"Agreed about what?" I ask, even though I'm pretty sure I know what she's about to say.

"We're telling the doctors when we get home:

it's time to turn the machines off." Autumn's eyes are green pools of tears. "My little brother's going to die." And with that, she falls against me and sobs so hard her whole body shakes. "I can't bear it, Jenni. My baby brother. I'm going to lose him forever."

I wrap my arms around her as tight as I can and try to stop myself from crying with her. She needs me to be strong — and I'm going to be whatever she needs.

"Oh, Autumn. I wish I could change things," I say as I hold her tight. "I wish more than anything that I could." Little Mikey. I saw him two days ago, right here. And now — it's unthinkable. It's impossible.

"I know," she says. "So do I. I've wished it every day for the last three years — wished we could have acted quicker at the time. Those three hours from when it happened to when he was finally scanned — how could a couple of measly hours make such a difference? Even one of them could have been enough to save him, enough to catch the bleed before it spread too far for them to operate. No one will ever know how much I've wished for those hours back — wished I'd never told him to gallop on that stupid horse and wished I hadn't believed him when he said he felt fine after the fall."

"Autumn, it's not your fault."

"I know. I know. I'm past that. I know it's no one's fault. And I know that no one can change any of it. You can't turn back time and make it all different. I wish you could, though."

That's when I realize. My arms suddenly feel heavy, and I let go of Autumn.

Can't you?

I've spent all this time thinking I'm trapped here for good—but there *has* to be a way to get back. There *has* to be. I might not be able to stop it from happening, but if I could just get back to the present day, I could get back to a reality where Autumn still has three more years with her kid brother alive. Let her live those three years again. And now that I know what's ahead, I can be stronger for her; be a better friend; be by her side, no matter what. We could spend more time at the hospital, look after him better; maybe we could even do loads of research, find something that could change all this—maybe even discover a way of getting him out of the coma. Who says we couldn't?

I've *got* to be able to do something. I've got to at least *try*—or Mikey will be dead next week.

"Jenni, are you OK?" Autumn's staring at me.

"What?"

"Are you OK? You've gone pale."

I pull my sleeve back to look at my watch. It's one thirty. In half an hour — three years ago — Autumn and her parents are going to get the news that Mikey's in a coma that the doctors believe to be permanent. I need to be with her when she hears this. We need to do the whole thing differently. I *have* to find a way.

"I've got to go," I say suddenly.

"You're leaving me? Now? After everything I've just said?"

I take both of her hands in mine. "Autumn, I'm not leaving you. I'm going to change things. Not everything, but some of it. I'm going to make it better."

"But how — ?"

"Just trust me, OK? Do you trust me?"

She nods.

"OK, I have to go, then."

"Jenni," she says softly.

I pause at her side. "What?"

She swallows. "I'm sorry. For everything. I'm sorry I pushed you away."

I smile at my best friend. "You don't have anything to be sorry for," I say. "Nothing at all. It's going to be OK. You'll see."

And then I run up the path, back to Autumn's

building. If I can just get back to the elevator, if I can find a way of getting into it again somehow. There's *got* to be a way. Things *can't* be stuck like this forever.

I'm standing on the fourth floor, in front of the old elevator. Correction, in front of where the old elevator used to be. But there's absolutely no sign that it was ever there.

Maybe there never was another elevator. Perhaps I really did lose my memory. Or imagined this entire thing. Maybe I really *am* losing my mind. I lean against the wall, letting my head fall against it. It makes a hollow thud.

Hollow. The wall's hollow. It's plasterboard! The elevator must still be behind it! Maybe I can get to it after all. I hammer against it with my fists. But it's useless. All I'm doing is bruising my hands.

I search frantically around me. Nothing. The place is always so tidy, so perfect.

Then I remember the closet downstairs with all the logs in it. Maybe . . .

I tear down the stairs. The place where the old elevator should be is exactly the same as the place on the fourth floor: sealed up, painted over, but hollow and flimsy. But it's not the elevator I want; it's the door beside it. I throw the closet door open. A couple of brushes are propped up along one side, a mop in a bucket along the other. I consider these for a second. Not heavy enough.

Then I spot it in the far corner. Bingo! The ax Mr. Barraclough used for the logs!

I grab the ax and run back up to the fourth floor. I've got to come back to the first floor in the elevator.

I'm panting by the time I get to the fourth floor. My chest feels like it's got rubber bands wrapped tight around it. I run to the elevator.

I've never done anything like this in my life. Jenni Green doesn't do things like this! Except, judging by today's events, it seems Jenni Green has changed. Autumn would be proud of me for what I'm about to do. Will I ever get to tell her? Would she believe me, even if I did?

I've no time to think about questions I can't answer. I've got to do this.

With a quick look around me to make sure there's no one there to see what I'm about to do — and a silent apology for what in anyone's book would amount to mindless vandalism — I lift the ax over my shoulder, take a deep breath, and smash it as hard as I can against the wall.

I've done it. There's a hole in the wall. Through it, I can see the metal door of the elevator. It's still there, behind the wall, exactly as it was.

I just need to reach the button. I raise the ax again and again, cracking it against the wall until I've made a gap big enough to reach through. I feel around on the old wall behind the plasterboard. That's it. The button. I press it and wait.

Nothing happens.

I've made a hole big enough to climb through now, but there's nowhere to climb to. Just the old door standing closed in front of me. What am I going to do? This is my one and only chance to change this.

I press the button again. *Please, please, please work. I'll do anything. I'll be the best friend ever in the world and the best daughter. I'll only ever think of others, never myself. I'll work hard at everything. Just please let me get into the elevator!*

And then I hear it. The whirring noise. I leap up. It's happening. It's coming! My heart's banging so hard it's hurting my chest.

I clamber through the hole, open the first door wide enough to squeeze through, then pull the elevator's inner door across. Without pausing to think, I close the doors behind me, slam my hand on to the button that says *1,* and hold my breath as the elevator rattles into action.

The elevator seems to creak downward even more slowly and uncertainly than last time, shaking and rattling all the way. It sounds as if bits of metal are falling down the shaft below me. Eventually, it rattles to a halt and I pull the gate across, open the outer door, and step out. The plaster wall is gone! I glance behind me to make sure the elevator doesn't disappear the moment I've turned my back. It doesn't. It's still there.

I check my watch. Quarter to two.

Quarter to two? My heart drops so hard it's as if it's falling down an elevator shaft itself. What was I *thinking*? I'm a complete and utter fool! There's no way I can get to the hospital in time to change anything. It takes at least twenty minutes to get there in the car. Half an hour if it's anyone except my dad driving.

And even if I could get to the hospital faster, what could I possibly change, anyway? I've been kidding myself — trying to stop something that's going to happen whether I'm there or not. I was so desperate to help, it didn't occur to me that the main thing I need to change is the accident — and there's *nothing*

I can do to change that. It's already happened, and there are no buttons left to press in the elevator. I can't go anywhere and I can't change anything.

The best I can hope for is that I can be a better friend this time around.

I tighten my belt to hold up the jeans that are baggy again, get back into the elevator, and slump down against the wall, my head in my hands. Maybe I'll just sit here in a ball, hide in this elevator, and hope it'll all go away.

There's a noise in the foyer as someone comes in from outside. I jump up.

"Jenni!"

"Craig?" Six-year-old Craig! Cute, silly, messy-haired, and gap-toothed Craig!

"*Thought* it was you!" He grins.

"What are you doing here?"

He nudges a thumb at the door. "I saw you from outside. I've been talking to the workmen. Mom said I could, remember?"

I brush myself down and join him in the hallway. "Come on. Let's go back to the condo."

Outside, I take his hand and try to act normal. "So what did the workmen tell you about this time?" I ask, ready to let him prattle away while my brain carries on being somewhere else.

"They told me all about what they're building over the road," he says, his eyes shining with excitement. What is it about construction that's so fascinating to six-year-old boys? "They're making a new building where we can play Ping-Pong and pool and foosball," he says.

"Great. What else?"

"Um." Craig presses a finger to his chin. "That's it." He swings my hand as we walk. "Oh, yes," he says as we approach our block. "They were telling me how that one"—he points back at Autumn's building—"used to be a hotel, and all the rich people used to come there and the servants used to live in the basement and you never saw them and—"

I stop and pull him around to face me. "The *what*?" My face has gone cold.

"The servants. You never saw them 'cause they—"

"Not the servants." I pause while I catch my breath. "The basement. You said there's a basement."

"Yeah, that's where they lived."

"Really?" I drop Craig's hand.

"What? What's wrong? What did I say?"

There's a basement! Maybe the elevator could take me there. But it can't — I've pressed all the buttons. There isn't one for any basement. But maybe I didn't look carefully enough. Maybe there is a way. "I've got to do something." I start walking briskly back to Autumn's building.

"I'm coming!" Craig runs after me.

"Go home, Craig."

"I'm coming with you."

"No."

"Where are you going?"

I quicken my pace. "I don't know," I say. It's true. I don't know where the elevator will take me or even if there *is* a basement. But it's got to be worth a try. It's my only hope — and I'm *not* giving up till I've tried everything.

"What are you doing?"

I ignore Craig as I scan the buttons: *4, 3, 2, 1.* That's it. I *have* been to every floor. My heart sinks heavily, dragging down my last shred of hope with it.

But wait. Maybe I *haven't* been to every floor. The piece of plywood underneath the buttons. Could it be hiding something?

I pull at it, but it's stuck fast.

"What are you doing?" Craig asks, craning his neck to watch as I pull hopelessly at the wood.

"Nothing. Leave me alone, Craig."

He shrugs and wanders off — but a moment later he's back.

"Craig, I've told you to —"

"Here, use this," he says. He's holding out a screwdriver.

I stare at him. "How did you — where did you get that?"

"The workmen," he says with the simple logic only possessed by six-year-old boys.

I grab the screwdriver, then I grab him as well and plant a big kiss on his cheek.

"Geddoff," he says, wiping his cheek with his sleeve, but also looking secretly pleased with himself.

I work at the old screws, and eventually I've undone them all. The plywood falls away — and I gasp as I see what's underneath. A cracked, wobbly button — and next to it the letter *B*.

The basement! There really *is* a basement!

Where will it take me? A year back? I try to remember what my life was like a year ago. Can I face going through the whole year again?

I don't even have to think about it. Mikey will be dead next week. I don't have a choice. This is it. My one chance to change all this — to *really* change it.

"Craig, go back to the condo," I say, shoving him out of the elevator.

"I'm staying with you!"

"You're not. Go home."

"No!" he cries, pouting.

I take a tight breath. "OK. But you can't come in with me. Wait here."

Before he can argue, I pull the doors closed and stare at the button till my eyes water and the letter blurs. I've got to do it.

The button wobbles and sticks as I touch it. Pressing it hard, I watch as Craig's face disappears from the little window and the elevator clunks and squeaks and whirs, taking me down to the basement.

13

Pitch-black.

I can't see a thing. I step carefully out of the elevator and crash straight into a box on the floor. As I stop to rub my toe, my eyes gradually adjust to the dark. I can make out a few vague shapes: boxes and planks of wood and overflowing trash bags everywhere. A giant junk room. I stumble to the opposite wall and feel around for a light, praying there aren't any rats.

Found it. A switch high up on the wall. I flick it on, and the room bounces into view as a fluorescent light flashes on. There's a steel door in the far corner. The only way out, it looks like. I head toward it, making sure not to trip over anything.

Please, please don't be locked.

It is.

No! One steel door, locked solid. I push and pull at the handle. The door doesn't move an inch.

I scramble around the room, lifting boxes, heaving trunks around, looking for something, anything that could get me out of here. I scan the ceiling. There's a fancy panel all around the top edges of the walls. An air vent, maybe? There's a tiny grille in one corner, too high for me to reach, even if I stood on a box — and about as big as my hand.

I slump down onto a box. There *must* be something; there has to be. I scan every bit of the room. Nothing. Not even a window.

"Craig!" My voice echoes around the room, fading back to silence.

What am I doing calling Craig? Even if I hadn't gone back in time, he'd be a whole floor above me. And if I've gotten my calculations right, he won't be there for another year!

I can't believe it. No way out. Well, there's *one* way out — back to the present. The elevator is standing open, waiting for me.

All this, and I've failed?

Wait! No. I'm *not* going to let that happen. Maybe

the old Jenni would have given up, but this one doesn't.

I'll think of something. Perhaps I can go back up and get Mr. Barraclough's ax, get through the outside door. Or get enough food and water to last a couple of days — long enough for someone to come down to the basement and let me out. Or perhaps I'll think of an even better idea. I'll do something — anything! As long as I can figure out how to get out of this building from the basement, I'll have a whole year before the accident happens. I can stop it — I can!

My heart leaping so hard it feels as if it's about to jump out of my mouth, I close myself back inside the elevator, and press *1*.

I'm going to do this. I'm going to change things.

I hold my breath as the lift trundles upward, getting slower and slower, the rattling and creaking growing louder and louder, the scraping noises spreading out into a slow screech. *Come on, come on. Get me back to the first floor!*

More creaking, clanking, clattering.

And then it stops.

I pull the doors across — to be faced with a gray brick wall!

The elevator has gotten stuck just below the first floor! Above the wall, I can see the floor of the foyer. If I jump up, I could probably get back up there.

"Craig!" I call out again. Where is he? Why didn't he wait for me? *"Craig!"* I shout louder. Nothing.

I grip on to the ledge in front of me, scrabbling up the wall and heaving myself over the top and out of the elevator. I clamber out, pulling myself up on my stomach. My jeans are covered in dust; so's my hair, but it doesn't matter. At least I'm out. I'm back at the first floor.

I get up quickly, just as a young couple pass me. They're smiling, their hands entwined. They look familiar. Have I seen them before?

I dust myself off in front of the ornate mirror. For a moment, it looks strange to see me as twelve-year-old Jenni once more. My clothes are loose again. My hair's back to how it was, hanging in long, ringletty curls.

I shake myself away from my reflection and focus my thoughts. I just need to stay calm. I can figure this out. I've got a few more days until we leave Riverside to come up with a plan to fix everything. I *can* change this. I have to!

The TV's blaring as I open the door into the condo.

"Craig, how many times do I have to tell you? Turn it *off*!" Dad's voice blares over it.

"Where did you go?" I ask Craig. He's sitting cross-legged on the living-room floor, fixing a car while he watches the television.

"What?" He looks up, confused.

Dad comes out of the kitchen. "Forget something?" he calls.

"Huh?"

He dries his hands and wanders back into the living room. "You'll miss them if you don't get a move on," he says.

"Miss who?"

Dad laughs. "Who d'you think? Don't you *want* to go horseback riding?"

My mouth freezes as a chill creeps around my face and neck. "Horseback riding?" I ask slowly.

"You all right, love?" Dad says, looking at me with concern as Mom comes into the room. Big, round, eight-months-pregnant Mom. "You've gone white."

"Mom," I gasp, turning around. Then I look back at Dad. "What day is it?" I ask, my voice hoarse.

"Sunday, all day," Dad says. "At least it was last

time I looked." He holds an arm out toward Mom. She smiles at him and strokes his arm.

It's happened! I've gone back in time. The elevator—it never made it back to the first floor. That must be it. I've gone back a day! One day. I look at my watch. It's ten to two. On Sunday! I've still got time!

"I have to go," I gasp.

"Crikey, where's the fire?" Dad says. "Hold your horses." He turns to Mom. "See what I did there? Hold your horses. Might have to write that down."

Mom smiles indulgently at him.

I run to the door. "Mom," I say, turning around before I go.

She looks up.

I take a breath. How am I going to put this so she'll take notice of me? "You have to take it easy today," I say. "Please look after yourself. Don't rush. Don't get stressed."

Mom laughs. "Stressed? I'm on vacation!"

"Really," I insist. "I mean it. Just go carefully, all right? I don't want you to go to the candle museum. Please. It's too much for you."

"A candle museum is too much for me? Jen, I'm only pregnant. I'm not—"

"Please, Mom. You're not *only* pregnant. You're eight months pregnant, and you need to relax. Please."

Mom meets my eyes as though she's looking at someone she doesn't recognize. Well, she wouldn't. She's never had a daughter who's put her foot down and told people what to do before!

"OK," she says eventually. "You're right. I've actually been feeling a bit more tired than I've been letting on. Maybe I do need to take it easy. Craig will be fine playing here."

"Good. And, Dad, you need to cancel your squash match."

Dad looks shocked. "Cancel my —"

"Dad! It's important. Come on. We all know you're no good at squash, anyway," I say with a big smile so he knows I'm not intentionally being mean. I need him to listen to me. "Dad, you need to stay and look after Mom — and you need to pick us up from horseback riding. Please."

Dad looks at Mom. "Do you know what? I think you're probably right," he says, stroking Mom's stomach. "I don't think a game of squash is the most important thing in my life at the moment. I'll phone Mr. Andrews now and tell him."

I let out a breath as I try to figure out if there's

anything else. I have to be prepared, cover all bases. "And, Dad—be early, OK?"

"Why?"

I cross my fingers behind my back, hoping no one will know I'm lying. "Just that Autumn said they usually finish the rides early, and we don't want to be waiting around too long."

"Oh, the glamorous life of a taxi driver," Dad says dramatically.

I give him a kiss on the cheek. "Thanks, Dad." With any luck, I won't even need Dad to come at all, but at least I know he'll be there—just in case.

I whiz upstairs to change. When I come down, Dad's just putting the phone down. "Canceled squash," he says. "See you later."

"Thanks, Dad. See you in a bit." I give him and Mom a hug, praying that the next time I see them won't be in the middle of any kind of disaster, and hoping neither of them has noticed I'm shaking.

Then I have one last thought. "Oh, and, Dad," I say, forcing my voice to sound as casual as possible. "On your way, drive by Mile End Farm, will you?"

"Mile End Farm—what's that?"

It's where the lady on TV said the accident took place—not that I could tell him that.

"Look it up," I say. "Ask someone — it's just some-where I've heard about and thought we might like to visit. Thought you could check it out and pick up some leaflets on the way. Please just do it."

I feel slightly bad about lying to Dad. But it's the best thing I can think of. And if he figures out that it's actually someone's private address and not a place to have a family day out after all, I'll just tell him I made a mistake. The important thing is to make sure he's there in case we need him.

Dad shrugs and gives Mom a puzzled look. "What-ever you say," he replies.

I smile at him. "Thanks, Dad," I say.

And then I turn and run.

Please let me get there on time. Please!

I've got five minutes. Two o'clock on the dot, she said. Please don't let my watch be slow.

I'm breathless as I reach her block. The car's there. The Porsche. They haven't left! I've never been so pleased to see a flashy red sports car in my life!

I hesitate for the briefest of moments by the eleva-tor. I don't dare do it. Not even the normal one.

I run along the hallway and up the stairs, my throat on fire. As I pause outside the door, a flicker of fear rushes through me. What if they're not here? What if it's Mrs. Smith again? What if it wasn't the elevator at all but something else, and Autumn's still—

"Jenni!" Autumn's standing in the door, grinning widely. "You just made it. Come on, Mom's taking us." She pulls me through the door.

"Where's Mikey?" I ask. I have to see him for myself.

And then he wanders out of his bedroom, electronic game in his hand, mouth pursed in concentration. I run over to him, kneel down, and hug him tightly.

"Eurgh! Geddoff!" he says.

I laugh. "He's OK!" I say. I can't help myself.

Autumn tips her head to the side and rolls her eyes in my direction, as if I've lost the plot. "Err, I think so," she says. Then she goes over and feels Mikey's forehead and tickles him under his chin till he giggles and pushes her away. "Yep. He's as OK as he'll ever be, anyway."

Mrs. Leonard comes into the hallway. "OK, are we ready?" she asks.

"Just finishing this game," Mikey says.

"You can play it later," Mrs. Leonard tells him. "Come on. We'll be late."

I stare at Mikey, then Autumn, then their mom. "Mikey's not coming," I say. "It's just me and Autumn."

"Dad just got a call from Mr. Andrews," Autumn says. "Apparently he's got a squash court booked and someone's canceled on him at the last minute, so Dad's going to play. Mikey'll have to tag along with us. Mom's going to see if he can come out on the ride with us. They have lots of horses, so there shouldn't be a problem."

I stare at Autumn. My insides have turned to ice. "You're kidding me." I don't believe it. I've managed to get back here, stop Mom from going out, *and* get Dad to pick us up — and in the process I've made sure that Mikey goes riding!

Maybe fate has decided what's going to happen to Mikey, and there's absolutely nothing I can do to stop it. Maybe that's how it works: I could go back in time a hundred times — and still achieve nothing. The same thing would happen to Mikey every time.

I think I'm going to be sick.

Autumn makes a face. "It's a pain, isn't it?"

I can't even reply.

Mrs. Leonard's on her way down the drive. "Come on, kids, we're going to be late. Mikey, leave your game."

I grab Autumn's arm. I'm not ready to give up

and let fate take over just yet. "Autumn, Mikey can't come with us!"

"I know. It's so unfair, but there's nothing we can do. He can't stay here on his own."

"He could go over to my house, hang out with Craig."

"I don't want to hang out with Craig. I want to go horseback riding," Mikey says, shoving past us and running to the car. "I've got the front seat!"

I clench my fingers into fists by my side. "Autumn, he can't come," I hiss. "We can't let him."

Autumn laughs. "Hey, don't get too worked up about it. It'll be fine; we don't need to talk to him."

"It's not that," I say, squeezing into the back of the car with Autumn squashed in next to me.

She looks at me. "What is it?" she asks, an edge of defensiveness creeping into her voice. "We do enough things with your family; why's it such a problem to have my kid brother come with us?"

"I — I can't explain. It just is," I say, scratching around for another idea. If I can't persuade her to stop Mikey from coming with us, I'll have to some-how pull the plug on the whole trip.

"Look, it's me, OK? I don't want to go. I want to do something else," I say. I lean forward, as well as I can manage in the tiny space, and tap Mrs. Leonard's shoulder. "Um, actually, I've changed my mind about going horseback riding."

Autumn bursts out laughing. "You're messing with me, aren't you?"

Mrs. Leonard glances at me in the rearview mirror. "Are you OK, Jenni?"

"No, not really. I feel a bit — um, sick. I don't think I can go riding. Can we do something different?" Then I remember today's trip. "Can we go to the candle museum instead?"

Autumn guffaws and punches me on the arm. "You're hilarious!" she says. "I love it."

Mrs. Leonard smiles indulgently at us both. "You two," she says. "OK, seat belts on — we need to get there."

And then she drives Autumn, Mikey, and me to the stables, and I can't speak another word all the way there. All I can think is: *I can't let this happen.* After everything I've lived through in the last couple of days, I can't have made it back here only to let the whole thing happen all over again. Only this time, it's going to happen in front of my eyes.

I'll have to think of something else. I've still got time. Maybe I can talk to someone at the stables.

Get them to call off the ride, say the horses are all sick, they haven't got enough staff, it's too hot to go out — anything! There's only one thing I know: I've got to stop Mikey from getting on that horse.

Autumn gets out of the car and marches ahead with Mikey. I trail behind with Mrs. Leonard.

"Can't Mikey stay with you?" I say uselessly.

"I've got a spa appointment, and then I'm meeting my husband for a hot date at the rec center after his squash match," she says, laughing. "Hey, what's wrong with Mikey all of a sudden? You've never minded him being around before."

We cross a dusty yard and head toward the far corner. A wooden RECEPTION sign is nailed onto the wall.

Inside, a bunch of excited girls are lining up with their parents. A woman behind a small desk is scribbling something on a form. She gets up to fetch a couple of helmets. Bits of straw litter the ground; a leathery smell wafts across the room.

Mikey runs over. "She says I can go, too," he says, grinning as the woman comes over to him with a helmet in her hand.

"Try this one," she says, handing Mikey the helmet. She looks familiar. Where have I seen her before?

As she turns to us and smiles, I realize where I've seen her. It's the woman from the news program!

My body shakes. It's going to happen. Soon—within hours—and no one knows it except me. It's still going to happen!

Everyone's acting so normal: smiling, laughing, trying on helmets. How can they do that? I can't just stand back and watch it happen, I can't!

Autumn takes the helmet she's offered and goes to wait outside in the yard. I follow her when I've got mine and we say good-bye to her mom.

"Autumn, please listen," I say, my voice low so no one else can hear me. I'm going to tell her the truth. I've no choice.

"Come on, Jen. Just go with it," she says, grinning as she fastens the strap on her helmet. "You never know, it might even be as much fun as the candle museum." Then she bursts out laughing.

I take a breath. "It's not safe. Something awful is going to happen to Mikey if he comes horseback riding today."

She stops what she's doing. "Oh, Jenni. Please don't do this."

"Do what?"

"Resort to sci-fi stories as a way to get me to listen. If you don't want to come, don't, but *please* stop trying to spoil it for me and my brother. Give him a break."

"Autumn, just *listen* to me!" I snap. "I'm not trying to spoil it for you *or* Mikey. I'm trying to warn you!"

"Warn me? So you can see into the future now, can you? What are you, a psychic?"

The woman from the stables has come out of the office. "OK, all those on the ride, this way," she says, striding off to a row of stables on the other side of the yard. Autumn hurries after her. "I'm Carol, by the way," the woman calls over her shoulder as she walks. There are ten of us. Four girls who look about my age, all giggling together; a gangly boy on his own, pacing awkwardly along behind them; an older couple; and the three of us.

How am I going to stop this from happening?

I scurry to the front of the group, following just behind Carol and Autumn. Carol stops at the first stable. "This is Hunter," she says, stroking his nose. "Very good-natured, easy to control, but powerful when he wants to be. Mark, you can take him; you've ridden before, haven't you?"

The gangly boy blushes and nods quickly.

Moving on, Carol casts her eye over the group. "Marion," she says, motioning the older woman to come forward. "You want to take Star?"

"Okeydoke." Marion smiles, tickling the horse's nose.

Carol moves on to the next stable. "Now, here's one of our new boys," she says, reaching in to pat the horse in the next stable. The horse jerks its head up, batting her hand away. It's got a dark-brown nose, a thin white stripe running down the center. "He's young, but he's a darling. He'll be suitable for one of the children. He can be a little feisty," she says, smiling, "but sweet as pie if you keep him in check."

Mikey steps forward. "I like him," he says. "What's his name?"

"Angus."

My blood runs cold. *Angus*. Mikey takes another step forward, reaching out to stroke him.

"I want him!" I burst out. It's him! The horse from the TV. The one that threw Mikey off.

"You?" Autumn snorts. "I thought you didn't even want—"

"I want him," I repeat.

Carol turns to me. "Can you ride?" she asks.

"Yes," I say firmly. Autumn opens her mouth to

speak. "I've ridden lots," I add quickly. "Please let me ride Angus."

Carol looks me up and down. "OK." She smiles. "You're about the right height."

She moves on, the rest of the group following her to the next stable. "Now, this is Mouse," I hear her say. She points to Mikey. "Same size as Angus. Not quite so spirited but loves trail rides. Want to take him?"

Mikey agrees. Autumn takes the next horse. She's called Winter. As the group moves on, she gives her horse a stroke before turning to look at me over her shoulder. "What are you up to?" she asks.

"I'm not up to anything."

"Yes, you are. Pretending to be all psyched when you don't even want to be here. What's going on?"

"I just liked the look of Angus. Anything wrong with that?"

I glance across at Mikey. He's still stroking his horse. Mouse nuzzles into Mikey's shoulder as Autumn shrugs and turns away.

"Come on, Jenni," Carol calls from her horse. Everyone else has gotten on and is waiting for me, surrounding me in the yard.

I try to smile as I stand next to Angus, gripping the bridle and praying he won't step on my foot. Carol jumps down from her horse. "Come on," she says. "I'll give you a leg up."

She reaches up to Autumn and hands her the reins to her horse. "You look confident enough up there. Hold on to Misty for a minute, would you?"

Autumn watches me as she takes the reins.

"Bend your leg," Carol says, standing behind me and heaving me up into the air. Oh, heck, she's lifting me onto the horse!

I'm up. High up in the air, clutching the reins. "Thanks," I say, my voice shaking.

"Adjust your stirrups," Carol says.

I look down at my feet. *Adjust my stirrups? How do I do that?*

With a sigh, Carol comes back to my side. "Bend your leg forward," she says, then yanks at a strap under the saddle. She walks around to the other side and does the same.

"You sure you've ridden before?" she asks.

"Yeah, lots," I say, forcing a laugh. "I just didn't hear you properly."

"OK, well, ride at the back with me to begin with,

so I can keep an eye on you. Angus can get a bit frisky. Just keep a firm grip on the reins, OK?"

"OK," I say woodenly. And then she's moving away and jumping back onto her horse.

"Walk on, everybody," she calls, waving the riders past her. She indicates a girl on horseback ahead of us who must work at the stables, too. "Sue will lead from the front. I'll stay at the back. The rest of you, stay in between us, OK?"

"You goof," Autumn says with a laugh as she passes me. "At least we're here, though. It's not all that bad, is it?"

"No, it's great," I say through gritted teeth.

Autumn laughs again before kicking her horse and trotting to catch up with Mikey, who's up ahead walking alongside Mark.

I copy everyone's movements, squeezing my legs into the horse's sides. "Come on, Angus," I say under my breath. "Be good for me." He pulls at the reins, stretching his head out and making me lurch forward in my seat before he settles into a steady walk.

We ride down to an old railroad track that's been turned into a walkway. Trees reach across the top, in a ferny arch. Flies buzz around the horses' heads as we walk along in a line, hooves thudding gently on the ground.

Angus is behaving himself perfectly. I'm even starting to enjoy it. It's easy. All I have to do is hold on to the reins and sit still. He does the rest.

"We're turning here," Sue calls from up at the front. I look to see where she's pointing. The path leads up through the trees to another path higher up.

"There are some lovely open fields up here where we can canter."

"Excellent," one of the girls in front of me says to the girl alongside her. "I thought we were going to walk all afternoon."

"Boring!" her friend replies.

The horses turn up toward the high path. "Come on, Angus," I whisper. "Up here." He stops at the bottom of the new path. "Come *on,*" I repeat. Nothing. He won't move.

Carol's right behind me. "Give him a kick," she says. "Walk on, Angus."

I bounce my heels against his sides the way I've seen the others do. Angus pulls on the bridle, yanking me forward.

"Steady," Carol says. She rides around to my side and tugs gently on the bridle. Angus jerks his head up again but still doesn't move. I grip the reins with sweaty palms. *Come on, Angus. Please don't do this.*

Carol gives him a tap with her whip. He gives one more yank on the reins, rearing up slightly before settling down again. "Give him a little kick," she says again. "Just gently. Use your heels."

I squeeze my heels into his sides, and he finally edges forward. As he follows the others up the path, I breathe a sigh of relief. My heart's racing.

The path takes us up to a wide meadow. I can't see the end of it. All I can see is green open fields. Is this where Autumn encouraged Mikey to gallop? A thought crashes into my head so hard it takes my breath away: *What if it happens to me? What if Angus gallops across the field and I'm the one who's thrown off, I'm the one who ends up — ?*

"OK, gather around me, everyone," Carol calls the group together, thankfully breaking into my thoughts. "Those of you who are happy to have a canter here can do so. We're heading over there to the stream and the woods." She points to some trees in the distance. "Hands up who's ready to do that?"

The group of girls raise their hands. So does Autumn. The only people who don't are Mark, Mikey, me, and the older couple.

"Mikey, you can canter — come with us," Autumn whispers.

"He's fine with me!" I snap, before he can reply. Autumn just gives me a funny look and starts to head off with the other girls.

"You go ahead with Sue," Carol says to Autumn. "The rest of you stay close to me, OK?"

I nod, holding tight on to the reins as I watch the others charge across the field, Autumn racing ahead at the front. Mikey's just ahead of me. Safe. I'm starting to breathe almost normally again. *Nearly there, nearly there.*

"We'll just take it at a steady trot," Carol says. "You guys OK with that?"

As we set off, I bounce around in the saddle, jigging and slipping. I hang around behind the others so they won't notice. Every time Carol looks around, I try to lift myself in the stirrups the way the others are doing.

"Just along that river for a bit, then down a lane to Mile End Farm, and that's our halfway point," Carol calls to us.

Mile End Farm! My throat tightens another notch.

"Sounds fine," I force myself to say. The others smile and nod.

As we approach the river, I recognize the surroundings. It's where they filmed the news report. We're near the farm now. *This is where it happened.*

They're all waiting on the other side of the river. Even Mikey's already gone across.

But I can't do it. The horse, Angus, he galloped up to the river, and plunged down the bank without slowing. That's how Mikey was thrown off. And now he's going to do it to me. It's all going to happen to me instead!

No. No, it doesn't have to be like that. I'm not galloping. I'm not Mikey. I've changed the past. I'm safe. I can do it.

"Come on, Jenni." Carol's calling from behind me. I'm gripping the reins tight, yanking Angus's head upright and making him dance jerkily at the water's edge. If I'm not careful, I'll make him buck me off. I've got to cross it.

Autumn's watching me from the other side, laughter in her eyes. Mikey is next to her, staring at me like all the others.

"Come on, Jenni. What're you waiting for?" he calls.

Why don't any of you understand? This is serious!

Then Angus makes his own mind up and walks into the water. I can't look. I've virtually got my eyes closed as he gracefully steps across. Two seconds later, we've done it. We're across! I want to scream and laugh. We've avoided the accident! I've changed everything! It's not happened to Mikey, and it's not going to happen to me, either!

I'm so desperate to tell someone. I wish Autumn would listen to me. All the things we've talked about, all the sci-fi stories we've shared, maybe she really *would* understand, if I could think of the right way to tell her. I'll find a way, one day.

As we head up the lane, I can feel my confidence growing. I pass a couple of the girls, making my way toward Autumn at the front. I'll tell her everything, I'll make it into a joke or something. I'll enjoy the second hour of the ride as we head back to the stables. It's all going to be OK; I know it is. Mikey's riding alongside Autumn, the two of them confident and happy—I feel almost as confident as they look, now that I've stopped the accident.

"Autumn!" I call her as I pass the rest of the group. I'm grinning, waiting for her to turn as I go around the outside of the two girls behind her.

"Jenni!" Carol shouts from behind me. "You're in the middle of the road!"

It all happens so quickly.

The car comes from behind me. Too fast. Tearing along a little country lane at about eighty miles an hour, zooming past, virtually scraping into me.

Angus jumps up, throwing his head high. I grip the reins. Mikey turns at that moment, to see what's happening. I can see the horror in his eyes.

Pulling hard on the reins, somehow I manage to get Angus to the side of the road. I'm panting, almost breathless with fear and relief. That was *so* close.

But then I look up. I almost see it happen in slow motion, frame by frame. Mikey's horse, spooked by the car, rears up like a rodeo horse as the car disappears into the distance. Mikey's face is sheer terror. He's slipping in the saddle, grasping the horse's mane, his body hurled forward again as Mouse plunges back to the ground.

"Autumn! Help!" he yells. Mouse is kicking out with his back legs now. Mikey's completely lost control.

Mikey. My throat closes up.

And then he's in the air. Mouse has thrown him off. One silent, almost calm, moment. And then the

worst sound in the world — a sickening thud as Mikey
meets the ground.

People are leaping off their horses. I just sit, staring openmouthed at my best friend's little brother
lying motionless on the road.

It's just like before. I can't speak, can't utter a word.

*All this. Everything I've been through, and it didn't
change a thing.*

14

$\mathcal{I}$ jump down from Angus and pass the reins to Mark, who's pulled up alongside me. Everyone's getting off their horses and crowding around Mikey. I join Autumn by his side.

"Mikey, can you hear me?" I ask breathlessly.

Then Mikey opens his eyes and frowns at me. "Of course I can," he says. And then he slowly sits up. He sits up! He's all right!

Rubbing his head, he carefully gets to his feet.

"Mikey, are you sure you're all right?" Autumn asks, holding on to his arm.

He shakes her off. "I'm fine, sis. No big deal."

A moment later, Carol's in front of him. "Mikey? Where does it hurt?" she asks.

"It's just my head. Just banged it a bit. I'm fine, honestly!"

I'm so relieved, I can't speak. I changed it—I really changed it. Mikey's fine. Everything's going to be OK!

And then something happens that feels sickeningly familiar, but I can't think why. Carol takes her horse back from Sue and walks Mikey's horse over to her. "Take Mouse back will you?" she says. "I think Mikey should ride back with me on Magic."

"I'm OK. Stop fussing, everyone," Mikey says. "I can ride back."

Carol shakes her head. "Just to be on the safe side." Then she helps him up on to her horse and gets on behind him. "We'll take it nice and slowly back to the stables. Follow me, guys. Sue, you bring up the rear this time."

She starts to walk away, Mikey sitting in front of her, all the others starting to follow after them. And I can't move. I can't speak. I can't do anything—because I've realized something terrible. Something I only know from the news report that will be on television tonight.

This is exactly what happened last time.

❧   🍃   🍂

"Come on, slowpoke. What are you waiting for?" Autumn says as she pulls up alongside me on her horse. We're walking up the lane by Mile End Farm. I'm trying to figure out what I can say to Carol, and what I can do to change this — even though part of me can't help wondering whether Mikey really *is* all right. He certainly seems it.

"That was close, wasn't it? Thought he was a goner for a minute there!" Autumn says with a laugh.

How can she laugh?

I'm trying to figure out how to reply when a car turns into the lane ahead of us.

Dad! He's here!

He pulls up and gets out of his car, just as Carol and Mikey reach him. They stop beside the car. I kick Angus on, to catch up with them.

"Hey, what's happened here, then? Got lazy, did you?" Dad asks Mikey with a wink.

Mikey grimaces at Dad. "I'm fine," he says. "Fell off my horse, so they won't let me go back on my own. But I'm OK, honestly. Just bumped my head a bit."

As I pull up alongside Carol and Mikey, Dad glances across at me and smiles. "Hey, sweetheart, you having a good time?"

A good time? Am I having a good time? I look across at Mikey. That's when I notice the back of his head, right below his helmet, is swollen up like a tennis ball. Suddenly I can see that things aren't quite how they seem. What was it Autumn said earlier? The surgeon's words: that the bleed had spread too far for them to operate because he hadn't been brought to hospital in time. That even one hour could have made all the difference. How Autumn wished she hadn't believed Mikey when he said he was fine.

With a shiver that shoots through me so hard it makes my whole body shake, I realize I haven't changed anything—yet—but perhaps there's still time.

"Dad, you need to take Mikey to the hospital," I say, my voice croaky and cracked with fear.

Mikey lets out a breath. "Please, can everyone stop fussing? I'm *fine!*"

"We'll get him back to the stables and see how he is then," Carol says. "He's safe here with me. We'll be back there in an hour."

An hour till we're back to the stables? That's too long! What can I do? I have to make them listen!

"Dad! Please. He needs to get to the hospital now!" I say. This time, the fear has turned to panic.

It's searing through my throat like fire. "Don't listen to Mikey. He's worse than he thinks. If we take him to the stables, it'll be too late!"

Dad gives me a really strange look. As though he doesn't understand me or doesn't recognize me or something. Well, he wouldn't. Here I am again, Jenni Green, the quiet one who doesn't make a fuss, barking orders at everyone.

"*Please,* Dad," I say. "I don't often ask things of you — but I'm asking this. Please listen to me. We need to get him to the hospital. Now!"

Dad looks at me. Then across at Mikey. Then he nods. "OK, hold on," he says to me. "Wait up a minute," he calls to Carol.

Carol turns around in her saddle.

"Can I just have a quick word with Mikey?" he asks. Before Carol can answer, he adds, "I'm trained in first aid."

She turns the horse around to face Dad, and he smiles up at Mikey. "OK, let's have a look at your head." Mikey turns his head around so Dad can see. The bump is so huge, I clap a hand over my mouth to stop me from gasping out loud. I don't want to scare Mikey. Dad lets out a sharp breath. "That's quite a lump you've got there, kid," he says.

Mikey doesn't say anything.

"Mikey, do you feel sick at all?"

"No, I've told you. I'm OK."

"Have you had a nosebleed?"

"Nope."

"Does your neck hurt?"

Mikey doesn't reply.

"Mikey, is your neck sore?"

Mikey nods. "Yes. Why? What does that mean? I just pulled it when I fell."

"I'm sure you did," Dad says calmly. "I'm just checking. OK, can you tell me where you are, Mikey?"

Mikey laughs. "On a horse," he says sarcastically.

"And where are you on vacation?" Dad persists.

Mikey stares at Dad. Dad stares at Mikey. All of us stare at them both. Mikey's face has turned red. "I'm at . . . I'm at . . . I can't remember what it's called," he says eventually.

Dad holds two fingers in the air. "How many fingers am I holding up?"

Mikey squints at Dad's hand. "Um . . . I can't . . . Wait a minute, hold them properly. You're moving them around."

Dad's hand is completely still.

"Can you tell me how many fingers, Mikey?"

Mikey stares at Dad's hand, his face gritted in concentration. "Three? Four?" he says eventually.

Dad walks right up to the horse and reaches out for Mikey. "That's it," he says. "I'm taking him to the hospital."

Suddenly, everything changes. Dad's lifting Mikey off the horse. Carol's jumped down, too; the atmosphere feels as though someone has shot a bolt of electricity through it.

"Autumn, Jenni, let's go. Can someone take your horses?"

Carol grabs Angus's reins as I jump down. Sue rides over to Autumn to take her horse. "We'll figure it out," she says.

A moment later, we're getting in the car. Mikey's in between Autumn and me, and Dad's starting the engine.

Mikey's turned pale. He doesn't look quite so fine anymore. He looks more like a scared little boy.

Autumn squeezes his hand. "Hey, don't worry, bro," she says. "You'll be fine. Everything will be fine. We're just getting you checked out."

I want to say something helpful, but I can't find

the words. All I can think is: *Will he?* Will any of this be fine? Will we get him to a doctor in time to prevent the future I've already seen? The future where Mikey never, *ever* recovers from this? Or are we all fated to go through exactly the same thing, no matter how many times I try to come back and change it?

Dad catches my eye in the mirror. There's a question on his face. *How did you know?* he's asking. *What made you think I'd need to be here?*

I haven't got an answer — not one that he'd believe, anyway — so I look away before he asks it out loud and I'm forced to think of something. I turn to Autumn. "It'll be OK," I say. "Whatever happens to Mikey. I'll never desert you. I'll be by your side; I'll do anything you need — you're never going to lose me. You need to remember that. We'll always be best friends, OK?"

Autumn gives me a puzzled look. "I know that," she says simply, with an attempt at a smile. And then I go back to staring out of the window, with only one thought: *Please let him be all right.* I say it over and over in my head, biting my nails so far down my skin is sore.

Please, please let him be all right.

I'm sitting on a plastic chair in a hospital waiting room, holding Autumn's hand. Mom's on the other side of me, and Autumn's mom on the other side of her. Our dads are walking up and down in the corridor. Craig's sitting on the floor, playing with his cars.

Mikey's in a room with some doctors, having his head scanned.

No one is saying anything. It's as if all the sound has been sucked out of the world, along with all the color and the joy. All that is left is this waiting. And the question going around and around in my head: *Did we get him here in time?*

"Tom." Mom breaks the silence. Dad and Mr. Leonard both turn to look at her. She points down the corridor. "The doctor's coming back."

At last.

Dad and Mr. Leonard rush back to join us, and the doctor comes over and pulls another chair over for himself. He's sitting down; that's not good, is it?

"Are you all family?" he asks.

Mom opens her mouth to speak, but Mr. Leonard beats her to it. "Yes," he says firmly. "Dr. Wilson, just tell us how Mikey is." He reaches out to take Mrs. Leonard's hand. "Please."

The doctor breathes in. "Mikey's had a nasty knock

on his head," he says. "The CT scan shows that he's had something called an extradural hematoma. That's a bleed inside his head."

Mrs. Leonard makes a strange choking sound. Mom claps a hand over her mouth. I shut my eyes. I don't know how I think this'll help. If I could shut my ears, I'd do that, too. Anything to put off what he's about to say.

The doctor is still talking. "He's being treated as we speak," he says. "As soon as we've operated, we'll be able to tell you the situation more accurately. But I *can* tell you that, barring any unforeseen circumstances, he should almost certainly make a full recovery."

"A *what?*" I yelp. Did he just say what I thought he said? He couldn't have. I must have heard wrong. I need to be sure. "Can you say that again?"

The doctor turns to me and smiles. As he does so, I can't help wondering if this is the very same doctor who saw Autumn and her family in the other version of this moment. Were they sitting on these very chairs? Did he smile at them that time, too?

"All our tests tell us that Mikey should be fine," he says. "He'll have a bit of a sore head for a week or so, and a great story for his friends — but that should be about it. If you hadn't gotten him here so quickly, this could have been very different. Another hour and the bleed could well have developed to a point beyond our control."

"What would that have meant?" Autumn asks.

Dr. Wilson shakes his head. "It's hard to say for sure. But, potentially, brain damage, coma . . . It could have even been fatal." He turns to Dad. "But thanks to you, Mr. Green, young Mikey should be just fine."

I look over at Dad. He's staring at me. His eyes are watery. I've never seen my dad cry. Ever. He tries to speak. Then he scratches his forehead and shakes his head. "It was Jenni," he croaks, eventually. "It was all thanks to Jenni."

Dr. Wilson comes over to me and looks right into my eyes. "Well, you, my dear, are a brave, smart, and lucky young lady. You don't even want to *think* about what this could have meant without your actions."

"No," I reply, banishing the pictures in my head of the world where I know *exactly* what it could have meant. I look back at him and, for what feels like the first time in about a hundred years, I smile. "You're right. I don't."

It's the last day of our week here, and there's something I need to do.

"I'm going to see Autumn," I say to Mom and Dad. They're sitting cuddled up together on the sofa, looking at a parenting magazine. Craig's playing with a miniature digger on the floor. I stop to look at them all. Mom's face is so content. Will it stay that way? Will *they* stay that way — in love, relaxed, *together*?

"Send our love to them all," Mom says, looking up from her happy haze. I smile back at her, and as I do, it's almost as if I can see the future in her eyes. And I realize that there's no reason for anything to go wrong, now that Mikey's OK. No reason for Mom to drive herself crazy worrying about losing a child. Mom and Dad will be just fine — I'll make sure of it!

I go over and kiss them both. "Will do," I say. And then I head over to Autumn's condo — in the normal elevator. There's no way I'm going in that other one ever again!

There's music coming from inside and a smell of incense wafting out. I smile at the signs of Leonard family normality as I knock.

Autumn's mom opens the door. "Hi, Jenni," she says, smiling. "Come on in."

Autumn's on the sofa sitting next to Mikey. They're watching a cartoon together. Mikey's got a bandage around his head and a very grumpy look on his face.

"How you doing, Mikey?" I ask, sitting down to join them.

He grunts something unintelligible in reply.

"He's so miserable," Autumn says. "His head's too sore for him to play his video games or run around doing anything interesting."

"Did they say how long till he'll feel OK?"

"Couple of weeks at most, they think. Then he should be totally normal again. Well, as normal as Mikey could ever be!" Autumn smiles at me. "One of the nurses said you were a heroine," she says. "I told her you're my best friend, and she said I'm the luckiest girl in America to have such a great best friend."

Her words are like the sunshine, warming me up inside.

"I told her she was wrong, though," Autumn says, a mischievous glint in her eyes.

My warm feeling evaporates on the spot. "Oh."

Then Autumn smiles so brightly, the room lifts another notch in color and light. "I told her I'm the luckiest girl in the WORLD!"

I grin back at her. "So am I," I say. And for the first time, I realize what being best friends means. It's not about thinking that she's the most amazing person ever, and I'm the luckiest person alive because she's my best friend. *No one's* the most amazing person ever. We're all just who we are. I still think she's wonderful. But I deserve her because — you know what? — I'm not bad, either.

"Best friends forever," Autumn says.

"Absolutely. Nothing will ever get in the way of that," I say, meaning it more than she will ever know. "Nothing."

Autumn flops back into the sofa. "So, what do you feel like doing today?" she asks casually.

For a moment, I hesitate. When was the last time Autumn asked *me* what we were doing? I don't think I can remember a time. Then I smile as I realize how many things I've changed.

I get up. "Follow me," I say.

Autumn jumps up and stands in line behind me. "Ooh, follow the leader. Fab!" I start walking across the room, and Autumn follows behind me, bouncing up and down in a funny walk that makes even Mikey laugh as he watches us.

I lead Autumn out of the room, out of the apartment, and out into the beautiful day. Across the road, Mr. Barraclough is walking toward the reception building. He gives us a quick wave and goes inside.

That's when I realize there's still something I've got to do.

"I just need to pop in there," I say as we pass the reception building. "I'll be back in a minute."

I've got to try it. I owe it to her, and to myself.

He's just inside the hallway.

"Mr. Barraclough!"

He turns and smiles. "Jenni, hi. How's Mikey doing?"

"He's fine," I say.

"Just a bandaged-up head, eh?" Mr. Barraclough says. "I guess it could have been worse."

"Yes, it could," I agree. "A lot worse." I fumble to reach into my pocket. "I've got something for you."

"For me?" Mr. Barraclough watches as I pull something out.

"It's a letter," I say. "But you've got to do exactly what I say."

He stifles a laugh. "Exactly what you say?"

"Please," I insist. "It's important."

I hand him the letter. "Read it now," I say. "On your

own. And then you have to go up to the second floor of the old building, condo 210, and take the letter with you."

Mr. Barraclough's staring at the folded pages. "Who's this from?" he asks, suddenly serious. "Where did you get it?"

"It'll all be explained if you do what I say. Condo 210, OK?"

"Right, right," he says, wandering away, still staring at the letter.

"Mr. Barraclough," I call after him.

He stops, turns.

"I haven't told you the most important thing."

"And that is?"

"Use the elevator," I say carefully.

"Yes, yes, if you insist." He turns away again.

"Listen!" I call after him. He stops again. "The *old* one," I say. "The one that doesn't work. Use that one." He stares hard at me then, as though he's looking for something more in my words. "Very well," he says eventually, holding my eyes. "I will."

We've been sitting talking and watching the weir rush by for the last hour. Autumn hasn't suggested we try to cross it. Even *she* wouldn't do it when it's this full.

She hasn't suggested we climb any trees or leap any fences, either. But even if she did, I wouldn't mind. The last few days have made me realize that I can do a lot more than I'd thought.

Autumn suddenly jumps to her feet. "Come on. Let's go."

Two people are coming toward us as we head up the path. As they get closer, I see it's Christine and Sally. "Hi," they say, smiling at Autumn and blanking on me, as usual.

"Come on, Autumn," I say, heading the opposite way.

"Oooohh, don't answer us, then!" Christine snorts, sticking her nose in the air.

"What was that for?" Autumn asks.

I shake my head. "I don't know. Sorry. I just don't like them. I don't think they're real friends."

We're passing the front doors to Autumn's building when there's a clunking noise from inside. Through the glass door, we see the old elevator being opened.

"I thought that one didn't work," Autumn says.

"Maybe they fixed it," I reply casually as two people emerge from the elevator. Mr. Barraclough — and Mrs. Smith! They're smiling at each other, lost in a world of their own.

Mr. Barraclough stops to hold the door for her, and they come outside. His eyes are radiant; his smile seems to light the space around them. I've never seen him smile like that. And I've never seen two people who look so much as though they belong together.

They don't notice Autumn and me. I guess Mrs. Smith wouldn't remember me, anyway. Maybe in her world, we didn't even meet.

But as they amble slowly up the path, Mrs. Smith looks back over her shoulder. Catching my eye, she smiles at me so broadly, I can't help grinning back at her. Her face is a mix of happiness, confusion, and gratitude. *She does remember me!* Then, when no one's looking, she mouths, *Was this you?*

That's when I realize — of course! Mr. Barraclough only went forward a year. She hadn't even written her letter then! I nod and give her a sneaky thumbs-up in reply. I did it! I really did it. I changed everything!

Mrs. Smith mouths, *"Thank you"* and smiles. Then she turns back to Mr. Barraclough. He takes her hand in his as they walk away.

Autumn nudges me and points to their locked hands. "Who's that, then?"

"Mr. Barraclough's wife, perhaps?" I say, smiling.

She gasps. "Wife? I didn't know he was married."

"I'm pretty sure he isn't," I say. "But I've got the feeling he might be soon."

We continue on up the path. As we walk along, the questions slip into my mind. Will I ever tell Autumn the truth about what happened? Would she believe me if I did? Would it make her angry like last time, or would it be the best secret in the world to share?

"Come on. Let's go to our place," Autumn says, and I remember the last time we went there. When was it? Yesterday? Last week? *Next year?*

And then I can't help laughing to myself as I realize that none of the questions matter now. The past is over and done with, and the future will look after itself. The present is all we've got—and, right now, it's all I want.

Autumn turns to look at me. "What're you laughing at?" she asks.

"Everything!" I say, looking around me at all the things that are back to normal. "The fact that the parking spaces aren't numbered and the ivy isn't too bushy—and your dad owns a bright-red Porsche."

"Weirdo!" Autumn rolls her eyes and nudges me

in the ribs. "How on earth did I get stuck with you as my best friend?" she asks with a laugh.

I punch her on the arm. "I dunno," I say, quickening my step as we cross over the bridge and head for our place by the river. "I guess you could call it good timing."

ACKNOWLEDGMENTS

I would like to thank . . .

my family, for all sorts of reading and listening and pointing out of things that they've done during the process of my writing this book — even though they've probably forgotten that they did most of it, as I did start writing it a long time ago!

Fiona Kennedy, for deciding that actually the book really was worth publishing after all;

Amber Caravéo, for helping me to make it the best it could possibly be;

Catherine Clarke, for still and always being the best, nicest, most supportive, and generally fabbest agent ever;

Jonathan Engler and Meliora Thomas, for helping me with my medical facts. (If I've got any wrong, it will be because I didn't listen properly. They know their stuff!);

Laura Tonge, for doing, saying, and being all the right things at all the right times;

The Candlewick folk, for being wonderful to work with, and for doing so many great things for me and my books;

and the usual writer buddies, for the usual support, encouragement, feedback, and general sharing of the agonies and ecstasies of this writing lark.